SLAY BELLS

A Vintage Mystery

Eunice Mays Boyd
with Elizabeth Reed Aden

First published by Level Best Books/Historia 2021

Author Photo Credits: For Elizabeth: James Studios (Madison,
WI); For Eunice – old family photo

First edition

ISBN: 978- 1-68512-058-0

Cover art by Laura Duffy Design

This book was professionally typeset on Reedsy.
Find out more at reedsy.com

.

*To the Johnson Family, Dawn & Jay and their children Travis &
Rebecca for more than 60 years of Christmas together. A special
thank you to Dawn's mother Margie Dearborn who started the
tradition. Ironically, Dawn & Jay now live in Mariposa.*
— *Elizabeth Reed Aden*

Review for the Vintage Murders Series

REVIEWS FOR *MURDER BREAKS TRAIL* (1943)

"No scientific sleuthing this, but a blending of clues, coincidences and concentration...A better than most brain workout."—*Kirkus Reviews*

"As pretty, suspenseful and smoothly written a mystery as I've read in a long time."—Chicago *Sun*

"... well-tangled murder plot... Good entertainment."—New York *Herald Tribune*

"An exceptional who-done-it, which won honorable mention in the latest Mary Roberts Rinehart mystery novel contest, has been skillfully built into a book that is hard to put down until the last page"—Philadelphia *Evening Bulletin*

Chapter One

Through the doorway to the hall (Honduras mahogany—how much had that door cost per square foot when he built the house three years ago?), Irving Pluit heard the strains of "Noel." The new television set, no doubt. Funny how sentimental people got at Christmas, he thought—some people, that is. He might be sentimental, too, if things were different.

It would be easy for another type of man to wallow in sentimental regrets about this particular Christmas—a day planned and looked forward to more than a decade ago. This was to be the reunion day of the little group of once-close friends who had gone through high school together. If only the others were willing to call it off, as he was. And they would be, he thought, if Mercy Marsh hadn't been so insistent.

"We must get together while Mister Northcliffe's in town." He could hear Mercy's light, quick voice as his wife Edith must have heard it on the telephone when she accepted for the Pluits.

"We must be civilized," Edith had said. What a multitude of sins that word covered. Of actual sins, in this group. Edith wouldn't know. Surely, she couldn't know… but the things they all knew were bad enough—so bad that one of them was now serving a prison sentence and having the reunion would be as

1

safe as adding a fuse—and lighting it—to a charge of dynamite.

Irving sighed and leaned deeper into the sponge rubber of his favorite easy chair. It had cost him a thousand dollars at Sloane's, custom-built.

None of the others, not even Drew Lang, the high-powered executive, could boast a house like Irving's. He looked about the room at the three birds in their custom-built cages brightened for the season with Christmas bells on red ribbons, at the severe draperies blending unobtrusively into the walls. They didn't look half the fantastic price he had paid. The radio beside his chair was worth every bit of five thousand, even though he only used it for the stock market quotations. He'd had his desk specially built to make him look taller, and it had set him back three thousand dollars. Only, of course, it hadn't set him back.

They'd done themselves proud, he and Edith, when they built this house. Now, if he'd married Adrienne Howell...

"Bastard son of a bitch!" a voice croaked behind him.

Fine sentiments for Christmas, but how could you gag a parrot? Irving glanced at the old green bird hunched in the cage near the huge globe with its inner light that made the world vivid and close, the world he hadn't yet seen.

He'd have seen a large part of it by now if he'd taken Adrienne's advice. Her face came back to him again as it had been at their last reunion—young and flushed with earnestness, blue eyes spark-bright, every short yellow curl quivering. If Mr. Northcliffe hadn't pointed out how much more quickly Irving could make money as a dentist than as an engineer...if the need to make money hadn't been ground into them all...

Adrienne had been right. Not about himself, of course, but about a lot of things. Look at their set of schoolmates now—with two divorces among them and the new marriage

2

within the group... with one of them in prison...with the rivalries, the scheming, and the hate... how could they have a reunion today as they'd planned more than ten years ago?

* * *

June was hot that summer in the pine-candled hills near Mariposa. So hot the day of the last picnic that Irving had prolonged the pleasantly chilly business of anchoring a bottle in the stream, of painstakingly bracing it upright. But he couldn't catch Adrienne's eye if he wasn't watching. He stood up, brushing off his knees, and turned around.

She and Mr. Northcliffe were talking by an outcropping of granite above the grassy bench where the others were shaking out a red and white cloth and unpacking lunch baskets. Adrienne's blue sleeves wigwagged with gestures and Mr. Northcliffe, standing with his fingers pressed together in five steeples, kept shaking his distinguished silver-winged head as if they were arguing about something they'd never be able to agree on.

Several times her face turned toward the picnic spot, but not far enough downstream for her to see Irving signal. He'd better stay where he was, though, if he wanted to get her to himself; their clamorous reunions didn't offer much opportunity for private talking.

It was good to get the Big Five and a Half together again, after four years of college, and see them starting out on the careers Mr. Northcliffe, their high school teacher, had helped them all prepare for. It would be interesting to see where they'd be in another four years, if the war America had entered didn't put them too far behind.

Irving knew where he'd be, barring accident; and Mercy Marsh, of course, would be a dress designer. His eyes rested on the black-haired girl in yellow, efficiently setting out food on the checkered cloth. Lately he'd been thinking of Mercy simply as the girl Adrienne was visiting, instead of the feminine Half of the Big Five and a Half, the one girl in their class at high school voted, with himself and Brooks and Drew and Red and Wally, "Most Likely to Succeed." Mercy would succeed; he was sure of that.

Brooks Chandler would too; he had a head start, with the Chandler money. Irving noted enviously that he could even afford to wear imported tweeds to a picnic. Perhaps, if Irving's own mother hadn't once been the Chandler cook, such things wouldn't mean so much to him, wouldn't make him resent so fiercely Brooks' certainty that being a Chandler would bring him everything he wanted without any effort on his part, resent even the way Brooks habitually stood, with his chin lifted and his hands—those large hands that weren't Chandler and that his mother was ashamed of—hidden behind his straight Chandler back.

Irving's eyes moved from the English tweeds to the tallest man in the group, the one with hair so blond it was almost white. He was standing at the water's edge a little apart from the others, drying his hands on a handkerchief, his head lifted toward the jagged horizon. Drew couldn't stand dirty hands, even on a picnic. Irving was kinder toward Drew than toward Brooks, for Drew's mother had run away with a mining engineer when he was six months old, and he'd been brought up by a stern father and grandmother in the knowledge that he looked like his errant mother, and in the fear that he might turn out like

4

her.

Drew would succeed because he had to.

Irving looked quickly up the hill where Adrienne and Mr. Northcliffe were still absorbed in argument—heated, apparently, on the part of Adrienne—before his gaze came back to Red Delorm and Wally Fleming. Wally—the tall, loose-jointed one whose black hair flopped as he extracted a banana from the fruit decoration on the cloth—would have any kind of success he wanted. Being one of the easygoing, impractical Flemings, he'd probably prefer a university professorship to making money, though Mr. Northcliffe thought he'd go far in criminal law.

Red's case was different. All the time he was growing up, he and his charming, irresponsible mother had been perpetual guests in other people's homes, while his charming, irresponsible father eked out a Hollywood extra's existence. By converting Red's doubly inherited charm into a bedside manner, Mr. Northcliffe thought there was no limit to what Red could make as a fashionable doctor. If he hadn't married Glenna...

Irving's interest, moving up and down the girl in green, brightened. Her family were Okies who'd drifted into Mariposa during the Depression. Glenna had gone through grammar and high school with the Big Five and a Half, and ever since the seventh grade, she'd been the most gorgeous girl he'd ever seen. Red was lucky, even if he never got to be a doctor, and probably he wouldn't be now. You couldn't go to medical school and support a wife like that in a way to keep her interested. And she'd better look out or she'd get pitch on that expensive dress from the pine she was leaning against.

Adrienne, on the other end, would help a man save money...

She was turning around at last. Irving's arm went up

to motion her his way. She made one last remark to Mr. Northcliffe and began to run down the hill, sliding recklessly on the dry pine needles. She looked excited, cheeks flaming and eyes a brighter blue than her dress.

She began talking before Irving could hear her.

"Why, that man—!" she was saying when he caught the words.

From the grassy bench where the picnic cloth was spread Wally bellowed, "Come and get it," and started toward her.

Irving sighed and began to climb the hill. There'd be no use trying to talk with her now.

He and Wally reached her simultaneously. The big man put out a big hand and took the other two each by an elbow. It would have been acting childlike to jerk away, and Irving already felt as small as Adrienne. It wasn't fair the way six-footers condescended to men who weren't tall—as if they had something to do with the genes they were made of.

Back with the others, Wally beat him to filling Adrienne's plate and coffee cup and collapsed on the needles beside her. On her other side, Irving pinched his lost trouser crease and strained his ears to hear what Wally was saying. He was giving Adrienne the why-haven't-I-met-you-before routine, and getting the appropriate response.

A good thing, Irving thought, that Wally hadn't met her before, that he hadn't been one of the people constantly running in and out of Mercy's shabby old flat in Berkeley, mined with dummies—and her feminine classmates—in samples of her dress designs. That was where Irving had found Adrienne. If Wally had been around, Irving never would have stood a chance. He'd thought more than once, too, what a blessing it was that handsome Drew wasn't interested in women and that Brooks, with all that Chandler money and poise, was taken with Mercy herself.

She and Brooks, balancing well-filled plates and cups, were stepping cautiously toward them across the needles.

"Did you people know that's one of my creations on that rock?" Mercy asked.

She motioned down the hill where Glenna had taken her lunch to a boulder overhanging the stream—a green-clad siren in the sun, with brown hair glinting gold and teeth blinding white as she smiled at Red on a lower rock. His long fingers, eternally tapping, played scales on one of her ankles.

"If you can guarantee all your customers'll look like that," Wally grinned, "you'll make a fortune."

"Most Likely to Succeed," Mercy said smugly.

"You will, Half-Pint," Brooks assured her. It sounded like the promise of a father to his child. He turned to Adrienne. "Can you imagine Mercy *not* succeeding, with her ability and drive? She's luckier than some of the rest of us."

"How can *you* fail," Irving demanded, "with the Chandler money behind you?"

"Look, Sawed-Off—"

"Look yourself," Irving snapped. "And watch who you're calling names!"

Brooks' small, even teeth flashed an imitation of a smile. "I don't like the implication that I can't get anywhere without my parents' money any more than you like to be reminded that you're not as tall as other men."

In the pause that followed, Adrienne said quickly, "Doesn't it do your souls good to see a couple as much in love as those two down there?"

The others' eyes followed hers to Red and Glenna on the rocks by the stream. The man's restless fingers still beat a tattoo on his wife's slender ankle.

"Remember in high school when Red sold his mother's diamond pin to buy Glenna a dress for the Senior Ball?" Mercy mused. "I think that's when I first realized you have to design women's clothes for men as much as for women—infant that I was."

Irving grinned. "I always wondered if Missus Delorm really knew what Red wanted the money for."

Brooks grinned too. "And I always wondered if Missus Delorm knew the pin had been sold until after it was done."

"He must love Glenna very much," Adrienne said.

"She wears clothes well," Mercy said, as if Red's loving Glenna was thus explained. "How're celestial mechanics, Wally?"

"Celestial mechanics?" Adrienne, too, looked at Wally.

"You behold a budding astronomer, madam," Wally said. "How long the bud will last without blooming will no doubt challenge natural science if the war keeps on. Celestial mechanics—"

For a moment, her dimples came out. "Don't tell me. It's more fun to think of grease monkeys with haloes. But actually, what can you do with a bachelor's degree in astronomy?"

"It's the first step toward a Ph.D.," Wally said. "And with that, if you're lucky, you can become a professor of astronomy one day—unless you want to make money."

Adrienne's cheeks turned a brighter pink, and blue sparks of excitement—or perhaps of anger, Irving thought—shone in her eyes again as they rested on Mr. Northcliffe beside Drew across the red and white cloth. "And making money must be mandatory for those 'Most Likely to Succeed,'" she said coldly.

Mister Northcliffe must have been giving Adrienne his "Money means success" formula when they talked this morning, though that could hardly produce the emotion Adrienne showed when she'd come running down the hill. They'd never met before, yet she was looking at him now as if he were a rattlesnake about to strike. It was funny how he always inspired admiration in other women. Mercy Marsh fairly sat at his feet. So did all the Big Five and a Half, for that matter. In his fifties, he was still incredibly good-looking, his body as straight and slender as Drew's, his eyes as unfaded and blue as Red's or Brooks'. But among his protégés, it was what he did for and with them that counted the most; never failing to bring his fine intellect to bear on all their problems, he always seemed one of the group himself. Adrienne couldn't know what Mr. Northcliffe meant to them, of course, but she didn't seem pleased with the good looks she could clearly see.

"I lean toward a professorship," Wally said, "but Mister Nortcliffe thinks law—"

She turned toward Irving, interrupting. "Do engineers make money, Irv?"

He took off his glasses and began to polish them with his handkerchief. "Some do and some don't. It's not necessarily a lucrative profession."

"I'm surprised Mister Northcliffe lets you take it then."

"Something tells me our Mister Northcliffe isn't a hit with Adrienne," Wally murmured.

Irving went on stolidly. "Engineering has certain advantages. Generally speaking, it's an outdoor life, and offers some scope for adventure." Then his voice lost its primness. "You can bridge gorges, change the course of rivers…"

He was seeing it all, seeing it as it might have been for him, if his plans hadn't changed.

A sharp, staccato clatter interrupted his reverie.

A few feet away, Brooks was banging two plastic cups together. "Hear ye, hear ye! I have an announcement to make."

Down by the stream, the siren and her earthbound lover looked up, Glenna still smiling, the sun illuminating Red's flaming hair. Across the checkered cloth, Mr. Northcliffe's silvered head and Drew's fair one turned.

Brooks set down the cups and straightened. Chin up, his large hands hidden, brown hair as neat as it would be in his mother's drawing-room, he looked as if he felt that he had been singled out first for the success predicted for them all.

"I don't know how you begin this sort of thing; I've never done it before," he said. "But I can't wait to tell you the good news. Mercy has finally broken down and agreed to become Missus Brooks Chandler."

Glenna jumped off her rock and came running up the hill. The others, too, got up and crowded about Brooks and Mercy. Drew, who had been looking like a sleepwalker all morning, warmed up enough to shake hands with them both, and Adrienne forgot her gripe, whatever it was.

"Are you as surprised as I am?" Wally murmured in her ear. "He's been crazy about her since they were kids, but Mercy—well, you knew her pretty well in Berkeley, I gather. Did you ever think she'd get married? The only men I've ever seen her show any interest in have been people like my dad and Mister Northcliffe."

The plastic cups were being banged together again, this time by Mercy, who called out as Brooks had done, "Hear ye, hear ye! I have another announcement. I want you all to know about the thrilling thing Brooks is doing for me. I don't need to tell you it's been the dream of my life to own my own shop. Well, Brooks is going to make that possible. Thanks to him, Mercy

10

Marsh, Incorporated, is going to become a reality."

Adrienne's and Wally's eyes met while a second chorus of exclamations broke out under the pines.

"I hate to think what I'm thinking," Adrienne scolded. "Mercy's not the only one tarred with the stick of money-grubbing. Everyone here except you sounds more pleased about Mercy's getting her business started than they do about the engagement. Of all the mercenary—"

Irving touched her arm. "Walk on down to the creek with me, will you, Adrienne? I've got to get something…"

They slithered along the bank of the stream. Once she slipped and he caught her around the waist, using the excuse of the slippery needles to leave his arm around her.

Around the bend, out of sight of the group by the picnic cloth, Irving stopped at the edge of the stream and brought up a dripping bottle of champagne. "Seven-forty a bottle. The best I could find."

"Oh, Irv, you knew about Mercy and Brooks?" Adrienne asked.

"I had a hunch, and thought I'd bring it along just in case," Irving said. "Besides, I was hoping…." He paused, and then burst out, "I decided not to tell anyone if I wasn't accepted, but Brooks and I both got on the alternate list, and yesterday they wrote that one of the fellows who'd been admitted had to drop out, and they've given me his place, and—"

"Irv, what on earth are you talking about?" Adrienne asked.

"Dental college," Irving said. "I'm telling you I've applied and been accepted."

"Dental college!" Adrienne gasped. "But you're going to be an engineer."

"I've changed my mind," Irving said. "And I've already got a half-time job lined up that's enough to live on."

"But I thought building bridges and things like that meant to you what designing does to Mercy," Adrienne said.

"There's more to life than chasing after dreams," Irving said. "And how could I ask my future wife to live in a camp? No lovely home. No clothes and jewels and—"

"You mean you think you'll make more money if you're a dentist?" Adrienne demanded.

"Well, sooner, anyhow," Irving said. "But wouldn't you want—?"

"What I'd want doesn't have anything to do with it," Adrienne said. "How will you feel in the long run about giving up the thing you've always wanted to do—to make money faster?"

"Adrienne—"

"It's that Mister Northcliffe and the propaganda he's been drilling into you!" she snapped. "Why, when I talked to him this morning it made my hair stand on end. Imagine you giving up engineering because you think you can make money faster at something else! And Wally giving up astronomy for law! And Drew, who can paint like nobody's business and wants to be an artist—your Mister Northcliffe wants him to use those talents in advertising!"

"Listen, Adrienne, you said what you wanted didn't have anything to do with it. But it does. Because it's you I want the house for, and—"

"Then for heaven's sake, stick to engineering!" she said. "I wouldn't want a house built with blood money. I wouldn't want—"

Irving caught her by both arms.

"Are you trying to say you wouldn't want me unless I stuck

to engineering?" he asked. "Or that—you wouldn't want *me*?"

In the suddenly still woods, a blue jay screamed.

"Oh, Irv, I—" she stammered. "Don't ask me now."

"I was hoping we could make today's announcement double," he said. "With champagne and all... but I couldn't get hold of you before lunch. What you could find so fascinating about old Northcliffe... it's not too late though, Adrienne. We could go back now and—"

"Please, Irv," she said.

"Please what?" he asked. "Go on with engineering?"

"Yes—that is, unless you really don't like it anymore. If you sincerely want to change, of course..."

"Will you marry me if I go on with engineering?"

"Oh, Irv, please—"

"That's just it," Irving said. "Suppose I get all set to bridge some river in the Andes, and then you tell me you're sorry but you love someone like Brooks or Wally, who've always had all the breaks, even down to knowing what to say when they introduce people. So you don't marry me after all, and I'm tied up in some gorge on a salaried job that may bring in enough to buy a government bond every few months, and—"

"But if you're doing the work you love to do, and making a good living at it, enough to buy gov—"

"Who gets rich on government bonds? How—" Irving began.

"That's all you want—money!" Adrienne said. "Money means success. Money means power. That's what your Mister Northcliffe—"

"Right, and I'm going to make it," Irving said. "I know a guy just five years out of dental college, and he's already raking in the shekels. Just coining money. He wants me to go in with him and—"

"Rake in the shekels too," Adrienne said. "Give up—"

"You're right I'll rake them in," Irving said. "Get a good practice and make smart investments, and there's no limit to where you can go. I'll build my wife a house she—"

"That wife's not going to be me, Irv," Adrienne interrupted. "I don't want you to get the wrong idea on that score."

"Oh, Adrienne, you'd fit the kind I'm going to build the way Brook's mother does hers. It's not because of my mother, is it? Because she worked for Missus Chandler?"

"You know I'm not that kind, Irv," Adrienne said. "If I loved you, I certainly wouldn't care what your mother did. But now I know how hard this get-rich craze has hit you... I wouldn't marry you now, Irv, even if I did love you. Forgive me for coming right out—bang, like that—but I feel this is too important not to know where everybody stands. You understand, don't you?"

"I know where you stand, all right, if that's what you mean," Irving said. His short, muscular body straightened. "Guess we'd better get back with the champagne while there's still something to drink it for."

The silent walk back didn't take long. By the time they reached the rock where Glenna had been sitting Wally, who must have been watching for them, stood up and came forward. Irving set his face in a smile and climbed toward the group beneath the tall pine, waving his bottle.

The rest of the day passed in a haze for Irving, a haze in which Wally kept his head glued to Adrienne's and only a few events stood out sharply. One was the way Adrienne jumped when Drew's shoe hit a rock as he bent over the stream for one of his numerous hand-washings, as if it were the crack of doom she seemed to be expecting. Another was the time her voice rose so sharply in the course of her long, drawn-out talk with Wally that Irving couldn't help hearing what she said.

"Oh, your precious Mister Northcliffe!" Adrienne said. "He sounds so tolerant and wise. And all the time he's actually a—a monster masquerading as Santa Claus!"

"My dear girl!" Irving heard Wally protest.

"But he is," Adrienne insisted. "He stands there making church steeples with his fingers, but butter wouldn't melt in his mouth. And the gifts he's bringing are going to backfire. You wait and see."

Wally murmured something Irving couldn't hear, and Adrienne's voice was heard clearly, again.

"He couldn't succeed, himself, in his own profession—not in a monetary way, and that's his only idea of success," Adrienne said. "So he's getting it through you, his favorite students. For all his friendliness and intelligent interest in your problems, and his gentleman-and-scholar air, he's leading you all around by the nose—and leading you right into quicksand!"

Wally said something that sounded like, "An A plus in Drama for Adrienne Howell!"

"I may sound dramatic, Wally," Adrienne said, "but I'm looking at the situation from the point of view of an outsider who's never come under the influence of your precious Mister Northcliffe. You're not able to think for yourselves; you're too fond of the man. With the values he's been pounding into you, what would happen if more than one of you went after the same thing?"

"But none of us are in the same field," Wally said.

"It's not just professional rivalry I'm worried about," Adrienne said, her face turning toward Glenna. "There are other things. What if you aren't all successful? What's going to happen to anyone in this Success Cult who doesn't make the grade?"

It was right after that snatch of conversation that Adrienne and Wally had joined the others, and Glenna had passed around the Cherry Snorts. Adrienne, of course, had to have the name explained—it was the Big Five and a Half's private name for the chocolate-covered cherries with—

"Just a snort of brandy," Wally confided to her. "A mighty small snort, of course. They're our special food." He put one into his mouth, chewed once or twice, and swallowed, grinning at Glenna. "No celebration of ours would be complete without them."

"We're talking about having the next reunion in five years, Wally," Brooks said. "Okay by you?"

"Let's make it ten," Wally said. "We may not be out of uniform five years from now."

Brook's face clouded. "The rest of you think you want to wait that long?"

"You should all be well started in your fields in ten years," Mr. Northcliffe said. "And I hope you'll ask me to the reunion. I'll be interested in seeing how you're doing."

"He means how much money you're making," Adrienne murmured.

"How could we have a reunion without you?" Red asked his old teacher. "You're as much a part of the Big Five and a Half as any of us."

Trust Red to find the right thing to say. His pleasant voice was smooth enough for any bedside manner, Irving thought; he was grasping at straws to keep from watching Adrienne. Too bad Red couldn't go to medical school, for Mr. Northcliffe was as right about Red as he was about them all. As right as Adrienne was wrong.

Their teacher was smiling at them now, standing so kind and alert, so much interested in them all. "I'd rather have you five boys and Mercy succeed," he said, "than succeed myself."

Living vicariously, Adrienne thought bitterly.

Brooks raised his voice. "Everyone who wants the next reunion in five years, say aye."

There was no sound but the breeze in the pines.

"In ten?"

Everybody spoke at once.

"The ayes have it," Wally grinned.

"Ten years from today then, if that's what you want," Brooks said ungraciously, and then warmed quickly. "Shall we have another picnic out here or would you like dinner at my house?"

"Let's not come back to Mariposa," Wally said slowly. "Our lives are going to take us all away. Why not meet in whatever city most of us are living in then? Thanks just the same, Brooks."

"Don't be so touchy, Brooks," Mercy coaxed as his face clouded again. "It's not that we don't appreciate your invitation."

"Some of us may not have the fare to Mariposa by then," Red added. "Glenna and I barely did this year."

"Nonsense, Red, of course we'll have—" Brooks began.

"Of course *you* will," Red said. His fingers were tapping now against the trunk of the great pine under which they stood. "You can't miss, with the Chandler money."

"I expect to succeed without help," Brooks said coldly.

"Of course you will," Mr. Northcliffe soothed. "You have brains, ambition, good connec—"

"Let's have the next reunion at Christmas," Wally broke in. "We're all more apt to be home then than in the summer, and thinking of the patter of little feet and dear old Santa fairly chokes me up. The ayes have it again?"

The ayes did.

"Mercy's got to get back," Brooks said stiffly. "She's going up to San Francisco tonight. Let's have 'Auld Lang Syne' and get going."

Wally held out a hand to Adrienne and a hand to Glenna. Irving moved farther away.

They stood there singing—the five men and the girl voted "Most Likely to Succeed," the wife of one, their proud teacher, and the lone outsider.

* * *

Irving Pluit sighed, shifting in his custom-built chair. He often thought of that picnic and the last time they'd all sung together under the trees. That year had been a big one in Pluit history; he considered it a turning point for him. In addition to starting dental college, with its accelerated wartime program, he'd met Edith McCrum, and after the McCrum influence had set him up in his first office, it had been one high, fast climb up the ladder. He and Drew had both been lucky that their careers weren't interrupted by being drafted into the service.

Too bad he hadn't met Edith before Adrienne met Wally. Then Irving could have ditched Adrienne instead of it being the other way around. But why use the word *ditch* even thinking about it? No sense rubbing salt in his own wounds.

For reassurance, Irving looked down at the tremendous rug on which his feet rested. Fifteen thousand dollars he'd paid for it—a bargain, at that. More than twice what Wally made in a year.

Yes, a lot of water had run under the bridge since their last reunion. That was a silly phrase. What bridge? One of those he might have built? He would have, too, if it hadn't been for Mr. Northcliffe.

Irving was surprised to find himself shaking. Shaking the way you do when you're furiously angry. Though why should he be angry when he thought of his old teacher or of the bridges he himself might have built? Certainly, he had made a hundred times more money by giving up engineering. It wasn't as if he had just one good dental practice; he not only had the office here in San Francisco, but three others around the Bay. Someday he'd have a whole chain of them, like groceries, in all the larger cities on the coast. But he wouldn't charge chain-store prices. Running four offices and making investments—he'd had wonderful luck with them all—kept him busy, of course. But what else did he have to do?

"Bastard son of a bitch!" the parrot croaked.

Irving glanced again at the hunched old bird that had started his collection. The McCrums and Edith's friends were always after him to build an aviary, but Edith knew he liked to have his birds about him and saw to it that the cages harmonized with the décor, and that the maids kept them clean. She wouldn't have them in her bedroom or the children's rooms, but her psychiatrist had told her hobbies should be encouraged, and the birds were always good for conversation when they entertained. The old sea-going parrot and the cockatoos from South America were the only ones in this room that Edith and the decorator called his study. Irving hadn't paid much for the parrot, bought in a moment of weakness when the call of far places had been unbearably strong, and he'd gone down to the waterfront to look at the dingy freighters with their foreign crews and foreign languages and smells.

"God Rest Ye Merry Gentlemen" was coming from downstairs now, accompanied bizarrely in the study by the parrot's forceful profanity. The music must have set her off. Too bad it hadn't been a foreign sailor who'd taught her to swear. Edith had been after him for years to get rid of the bird, ever since little Irving was old enough to talk, but Irving *pere* felt for the old parrot the nearest thing to affection he had ever known. Perhaps his birds really did do for him what Edith's mother was always yapping about—kept him in touch with the jungles he'd given up by not pursuing engineering. Adrienne was just being nasty when she said he wanted to see one more live thing in a cage that was smaller than his was.

His eyes moved to the red and blue cockatoos. That blue one was the bird he ought to get rid of. He could never see it without thinking of Glenna—the turn of its head, the curved flow of its smooth blue feathers. If he didn't think about something else he'd have to buy Edith another diamond bracelet. But his eyes kept flickering back to the blue cockatoo. It would take more than money now to tempt Glenna.

"Irving."

There was Edith, standing in the doorway, watching him. Now it did mean another diamond bracelet. But she wasn't a mind reader. Or had he ever told her who the cockatoo reminded him of? For that matter, what reason did he have to think she'd ever known about him and Glenna? It hadn't lasted long—or not long enough, at least—and Edith had never said anything.

"Mother just rang up," she told him. "She and Dad can't make it for cocktails before we have to go on to Mercy's reunion dinner, so with the Hardwick-Smiths down with the flu and the Waldos called to Washington, it's going to be a pretty small crowd here this afternoon."

"Can't you ask someone else?" Irving asked. "That's your department, Edith. Why come to me?"

"I wonder if you'd like to ask the Langs."

"The Langs?"

"Drew and Glenna."

Glenna Lang... he wasn't used to thinking of her yet as Glenna Lang. Of course, he'd have to see her at Mercy's...

"They're both old friends of yours, and on Christmas Day it's so hard to find people free. Would you rather have the Flemings?"

He'd have to see them too—have Adrienne tell him he was in a cage, and look smarter than his wife in clothes that hadn't cost a tenth of what he paid for Edith's...

"There's Brooks Chandler, of course," Edith said. "Only I've already asked Mercy Marsh."

"For goodness sake, don't have them together, Edith," Irving said. "Someone may try to introduce them again. I'll never forget how Brooks looked when Mercy smiled sweetly at that Hardwick-Smith woman and said, 'Yes, I used to be married to him.'"

"But we've got to be civilized, Irving."

Civilized again!

"If I were Brooks, I'd never be able to stick that reunion dinner—hearing Mercy's cracks at their marriage and seeing how far she's gone on the start the Chandler money gave her."

"She told me he refused," Edith said, "but she seemed positive she could make him come."

"What's she going to do—bribe him?" Irving said. "Brooks would do a lot for money now, even swallow Chandler pride, as I saw him do the other day."

"If I were Mercy, I'd be afraid to ask him; he's been so bitter about the divorce and her using up his money," Edith said.

"Afraid of what, for God's sake?" Irving asked.

Her hazel eyes strained in their sockets. "I never saw anyone hate someone else the way Brooks hates Mercy. Why, he might even shoot her."

"Then all the guests should be searched for guns," Irving said. "As far as I can see, everyone hates everyone in that group now. What a wonderful reunion!"

"Oh, Irving."

"Brooks won't come, and Red Delorm can't," Irving said. "Even Mister Northcliffe, the guest of honor, is so busy not knowing which of his five references to hate that he hates us all."

"What on earth are you talking about?" Edith's eyes were still bulging.

"Didn't I tell you he was trying to get the directorship of that citizens' committee on juvenile delinquency?" Irving asked. "They hadn't gotten what they wanted from professional surveys, so they didn't want any social welfare people or psychologists on this one. They preferred to put their money on some old-time teacher to give general direction to their untrained nosing. They were offering good money, and the committee asked for enough references to form a subcommittee. Mister Northcliffe, in his innocence, gave the names of the five Bay Area residents he knew best; three that meant something—Drew, Mercy, and me—and two that might have meant something once in Mariposa—Brooks and Wally. To make a long story short, the job's not yet filled, but he didn't get it, and gossip says his references queered him."

"But Irving, surely his five old students who were all so crazy about him—" Edith began.

"You know how hate thrives in that group," Irving said. "One or more of his favorite students must not have loved their dear old teacher."

"What a shame!" Edith said. "A job like that would have brought him all kinds of prestige. And with his looks and all... at least I know you wouldn't try to keep him from getting it."

"Money and prestige both. On a national scale, too, if the survey was successful. No wonder the old boy's bitter, after spending all his life teaching school in a small mountain town. Another angle, Edith, to add to the joys of tonight's reunion."

"Oh, Irving," she said again.

Poor old Edith looked upset. Her dark hair had slipped from its moorings and her mouth had gone white around the bluish lipstick. Her teeth were really good, even if the upper incisors protruded a little. After all, she couldn't help it if she wasn't as smart as Adrienne or as—call it alluring—as Glenna. Still, Edith was doing her best to be a good hostess, to provide the background he needed...

"Okay, ask the Langs for this afternoon," Irving said. "At least we'll go fortified. And, by the way, Edith—" He stood up, not too agilely for a man of thirty-two—he was heavy for his height—and moved self-consciously away from her. Not until he'd reached the cage did he realize he was walking toward the blue cockatoo. "There's a diamond bracelet I saw at Shreve's..."

He broke off. *Don't look at the curve of that damn blue breast...*

"Oh Irving, you don't need to do that," Edith said. Her high McCrum voice was almost warm. "Not after that pretty silver mink stole you gave me this morning."

"That's not enough, Edith," Irving said. "I told my secretary to get you something nice in fur, and I thought she'd get you a coat. That little handful of skins looks like she was trying to save the boss money."

"Not at all. It's beautiful." Edith's voice had lost its brief warmth. "However, if you want to be extravagant..."

"Of course I do, my dear," Irving said. "I'll order the bracelet in the morning. Then it's settled—you'll ask the Langs."

Edith was moving toward the door. "I'll ring them up now," she said. "And remember, Irving—not too many hors d'oeuvres, and no plum pudding at dinner. Remember what Wally said."

Better look out, Irv, or you won't be able to get close enough to a patient to fill a tooth.

He watched his wife go through the door and thought of the first time Glenna Delorm—she wasn't Glenna Lang then—had come to his San Francisco office. No one else knew she had one tooth in her head that wasn't her own; that was their secret, and the most rewarding bridge he'd ever built. It was after Red Delorm had been sent up...

The character of the Christmas music coming through the door had changed. The notes of "Jingle Bells"—thin piano notes—were unsupported by orchestration. He knew without going upstairs that the tune wasn't being played by his daughter, for whom he was paying out good money on piano lessons every week. It was Irving Junior, who wanted to be the musician in the family. Irving Junior, who was scared of guns, and who crossed the street when he saw a bigger boy coming. Irving Senior got up and slammed the hall door.

Instantly his gaze jumped up to the blue cockatoo. He walked toward the cage. There'd been talk, even before Red was convicted, about Glenna and Brooks. That was after Mercy had left him and taken back her maiden name, and the people with real money had begun to go in for Mercy Marsh clothes. Brooks had kept the apartment and been looking pretty down in the mouth. Then he'd suddenly improved. That was before the Pluits' new house had been built. They'd been living on 20th Avenue within a stone's throw of Brooks and the Delorms. Perhaps if they hadn't been so close, Brooks and Glenna… or he and Glenna, for that matter.

At least, short and paunchy as some considered him, and the son of the Chandlers' former cook, Irving had the satisfaction of taking the class beauty away from Brooks.

What would it be like to have her in his house as the wife of Drew Lang? It was funny to imagine Drew having a wife, let alone having that wife be Glenna…

Irving put his hand on the cage of the blue cockatoo.

At the click of a latch, the heads of all three birds and their owner turned toward the door. But it wasn't Edith, reporting on her call to the Langs. It was a red-suited, red-capped, red-mittened, black-booted Santa Claus, complete with mask and white whiskers.

"Bastard son of a bitch!" the sea-going parrot croaked.

"You taught him that?" Santa Claus asked.

"The children are upstairs," Irving said. "We've had the tree, but I'm sure—"

"I didn't come to see the children, Irv," Santa Claus said. "I came to see you. Excuse me, I should have said Irving. I remember you like both barrels."

Behind his glasses, Irving's stare grew more intent.

The Santa Claus figure stood swinging his bulging brown bag. "Santa's records go back farther than the present generation of children," he said. "I know where you used to hang your stocking—by an air-tight stove in an air-tight room in an old house in Mariposa that was built soon after the Gold Rush, and your stocking was always filled with fruit and nuts and candy from the Chandlers, and cookies Wally Fleming's mother baked. If your mother wasn't too hard up there'd be a quarter in the toe. I know—"

"Okay, so you knew me when," Irving said. "I thought your voice sounded familiar."

"But not as familiar as you'd like," Santa Claus said. "You can't quite place it. The mask changes the sound just enough. Mind if I set my pack on this chair?" He chose the custom-built nest his host had recently left, and slapped his mittens together. "Cold outside for San Francisco, isn't it? More like Mariposa."

Irving moved away from the blue cockatoo's cage. "If you want to talk over old times, why don't you sit down and take off your mask so I'll know who I'm talking to."

"That's only part of my purpose in coming today," Santa Claus said. "Though, as you say, Christmas is a sentimental time. Or did somebody else say that?"

"I'm not a sentimental man," Irving said dryly.

"So I've noticed." The other's voice was dry, too. "But I don't think I'll take off my mask. Then if I should get a little sentimental, neither of us will be embarrassed."

Irving sat down in the well-padded swivel chair at his desk. Keep him talking, and the man in the Santa Claus costume would give himself away before he knew it. Already, more than once, Irving had almost been able to say who it was. At first, he'd thought it was Wally. Then he'd thought Brooks. Once or twice he'd even thought...

"Pull up a chair," Irving invited.

"And put my cards on the table?" Santa Claus said. "No thanks. From now on I'm playing them close to my chest." The red figure paused by the globe almost shoulder-high on its bleached mahogany stand. "Way up north in the land of ice

26

and snow lies Santa Claus land," he murmured. "But Santa's in California now, in the palatial and highly decorated home of the Irving Pluits. How much did that desk cost, Irving?"

Irving named the sum.

"Not counting sales tax, I suppose," Santa Claus said. "It's a far cry, isn't it, from the early Gold Rush treasures your mother had in Mariposa. How much was that handsome globe where I just found my cozy little North Pole snuggery?"

Irving named the sum also.

"Not counting sales tax either, I presume," Santa Claus said. "Well, it's a far cry, and so forth. How much do your bird cages usually run you? They look pretty palatial and highly decorated too."

"Look here—" Irving's face was turning purple. "If you're trying to be funny—"

"Nothing could be further from my thoughts. I simply wondered if the little trinkets I have for the children..." The Santa Claus figure gestured toward his pack. "And I was thinking of old times and the contrast."

"So I gathered," Irving said. He wasn't practiced in sarcasm, although he'd been the butt of others' on occasion—of Mercy's, of Brooks' now and then, even of Mr. Northcliffe's when his inner promptings made him lash out. There was something about this man in the Santa Claus suit that reminded Irving of Mr. Northcliffe.

Santa chuckled. Perhaps it was the mask that took away the sound of gaiety it should have had. "You know what day this is, Irving?"

"Yes, Santy, it's Christmas," Irving piped. He was really in good form; he ought to do this sort of thing more often.

"Christmas, yes, and Reunion Day for the Big Five and a Half.

Remember the plans made at their last reunion, in the Mariposa hills ten years ago?"

"If you know as much about my Mariposa days and Mariposa friends as you pretend, Santa Claus, you know all about the reunion tonight," Irving said.

"Do you really think what Mercy Marsh has arranged fills the bill as a reunion, Irving?"

"It's the best that can be done, under the circumstances," Irving said.

"That's the joker—the circumstances," Santa said. "The shadow of San Quentin falls not only on the inmates but on those who sent them there. How could Red break bread with Drew and Mercy?"

"He won't get the chance," Irving said coldly.

"How, for that matter, could he break bread with you, who refused to lend him the money that would have covered his shortage before it was discovered?" Santa asked. "And Glenna... Red may have misappropriated funds from Drew and Mercy while he handled their accounts, but how many of the Big Five and a Half have misappropriated Glenna. Even Wally—"

"Wally Fleming's never looked at any other woman since he met Adrienne," Irving said sharply.

"I wasn't accusing him of misappropriating Glenna," Santa said. "But remember that lawyer friend of his he talked into taking Red's case for free? Remember the stories that went around about that lawyer and Glenna?"

Irving nodded.

"I understand there was truth to those stories and Red found out, so now he's gunning for Wally along with you and Drew and Mercy."

"But it wasn't Wally who—"

"It was Wally's arrangements with the lawyer that put Glenna under obligation," Santa said.

"But, good—!"

"Glenna didn't get mixed up with other men until Red was arrested," Santa said. "And now, since divorce for a felony is legal in California, she's married to another man. That stay in the penitentiary cost Red his wife, and he's gunning for everyone who sent him there or contributed to her straying."

"I wish you wouldn't keep using that word *gunning*," Irving said, "as if Red were free, with a gun in his hands."

"I don't know about the gun, but I don't wonder it makes you nervous—you and Drew and Mercy and Wally."

"What do you mean, *you don't know about the gun*?" Irving asked.

For a moment the study was still. Then Irving's visitor said, "You haven't heard about Red?"

"Heard what about him?" Irving asked.

The red-clad figure stood, legs parted, mittened hands behind his back, the Santa Claus face, with its rosy cheeks and permanent twinkle, turned without speech toward Irving Pluit. At last, a voice came from behind the mask. "He got out this morning for good behavior."

In the stillness of the room, the parrot squawked, "Bastard son of a bitch."

"Bastard son of a bitch yourself," Irving growled. But this man couldn't be Red...he couldn't...or could he? There were phrases... intonations...

The parrot muttered in his cage, this time unintelligibly, and Irving heard a faint sound like distant galloping. Across from him the Santa Claus figure stood with both hands on the desk. The backs of the red mittens moved in rhythm as if the fingers inside were playing scales. Red's habit...

"Who are you, anyway?" Irving's croak sounded like the parrot's.

Santa disregarded his question. "Red's is the most spectacular case, but look at Mister Northcliffe! Look at Brooks! Look at Drew, who may know his wife's been passed around! And you call it a reunion."

Irving sat silent in his place at the desk. He was thinking of the day, barely two weeks ago, when he'd met Brooks, Drew, and Wally at the Palace for lunch. It was Wally's idea to get together to discuss ways of helping Red when he got out. Good behavior would shorten his sentence (none of them had any idea by how much) or he might be paroled. Wally, in his impractical way, felt they all had some responsibility toward Red, and no matter what had happened, it was up to them to help him make a new start.

After they'd had cocktails and been seated at the table, Brooks made the astounding suggestion that Drew take him into partnership. While the other three stared, Brooks had smiled in his confident way and said, "Of course, I can't put much money in at first; you know Mercy left me pretty well strapped. But whatever price you set will be fair, Drew, and can be deducted from my share of the profits. Of course, I'd expect the Chandler name to bring in more business."

It was a full minute before anyone spoke. Wally, who had as little business sense as a man could get along with, spoke first. He said persuasively, "You don't want to do that, Brooks. You haven't had enough experience in advertising."

Irving was more blunt. "I'll talk with you about it later, Brooks, when we're alone."

For the first time, Brooks looked doubtful. "I thought Wally and Irving would back me up, make you see it my way."

Wally said something about Red, and they all (except Brooks) argued back and forth without deciding anything.

Brooks left first, and because the others stayed he claimed that Irving and Wally had influenced Drew to refuse Brooks' offer. Because Drew, of course, had refused. He told Glenna, and Glenna told Mercy, and Mercy told Edith, that Brooks turned livid in Drew's office when he got his reply, that he raved for half an hour about the Big Five and a Half's jealousy of him for being a Chandler. He claimed that they wanted him to fail. He swore that Irving and Wally and Drew were jackals gathered at Mercy's kill, and did a lot of fancy name-calling before Drew could calm him down.

Irving hoped that Mercy was wrong about her ability to make Brooks come to the reunion. After losing her and the Chandler money, he had bounced from job to job. Now, believing that even his old friends had rejected him, how could he face them all at the reunion?

Reunion... the man across the desk, his fingers still tapping in his mittens, was right—dinner at Mercy's tonight would be rife with envy, suspicion, and hate. It only needed Red to come with a gun...

As if he could read Irving's thoughts, the man in the Santa Claus suit spoke aloud six names. "Irving, Brooks, Mercy, Drew, Wally, and Red—the Big Five and a Half (not to mention Mr. Northcliffe)—the six 'Most Likely to Succeed.' You're tied together like a family, and that tie's as close as the tie of blood. You owe Wally's mother for the only real home life you ever saw, and Drew for your only glimpse of art. You borrowed the money from Brooks to pay for dental college, and—"

"That was paid back years ago," Irving said.

"What if it was?" Santa said. "The bond's still there—the things that can never be forgotten. You remember, Irving, how Glenna feels in the dark, and Brooks remembers Mercy. She and Drew may have played the most direct parts in sending Red to prison, but how large a part did Drew's wife play in making him steal? Or Mercy again, in making Glenna want Mercy Marsh clothes? Or Brooks by filling Red's outstretched hand when they were kids? What part did you play by not lending Red the money he needed? You've overcharged at the office, bragged about the prices you've paid for the things in your house, and on your wife's back— rubbed less successful men's noses in the dirt of their own inadequacy... How much do all of you owe to Mister Northcliffe, who taught you success was necessary?"

"Bastard son of a bitch," the parrot croaked.

Irving found he was shaking again with his earlier fury.

"It was Mister Northcliffe who kept you from seeing the Andes, Irving, from seeing Tibet and Arabia and Cyprus, from building bridges, or clearing jungles, or bringing water to the desert. It was Mister Northcliffe who turned the key in the padlock that chained you to a dental chair."

The score was even now, Irving reflected. He knew what the answer had been when the citizens' committee checked one reference. Just a little implication about the older man's honesty...

"How you must all be looking forward to this reunion," Santa Claus said. No wonder he didn't want to take off his mask. He could hardly stand there as Drew or Brooks or—Irving's throat tightened—Red, and say the things he'd been saying.

The silence seemed suddenly heavy, as if it had corporeal weight that was pressing against Irving's throat.

The beaming Santa Claus face turned toward him...no change of expression, no matter how bitter the words coming from those upcurved, white-whiskered lips... no knowing who was behind it...

"What's the matter, Irving?" Santa said. "Are you thinking about the far-off places you're never going to see?"

It didn't have to be Red. That notion was prompted by—*Face it, Irving*—a guilty conscience. Wally used to be full of silly tricks when they were kids. Perhaps it was Wally. The pressure on Irving's throat relaxed.

"Or are you thinking that it isn't too late to mend your ways, that you can learn to give your patients honest value—shall we say 'a tooth for a tooth?' That you—"

Irving jumped to his feet. "You've gone far enough. Why everyone thinks the dental profession is funny—"

Santa raised a mittened hand. "You're quite right; I've gone far enough."

"If this is a practical joke—"

"It may or may not be practical, Irving, but I can assure you it isn't a joke," Santa said. "Sit down and talk a few more minutes. There'll be only a few. You wouldn't turn down Santa Claus on Christmas, would you?"

So now it was the sentimental appeal! The costumed figure stood steepling his hands, for all the world like Mr. Northcliffe. It was maddening not knowing who was behind that mask. But if it wasn't Wally, it had to be Drew or Brooks or Mr. Northcliffe—one of the old Mariposa gang. Irving tried to forget that Red had been one of that gang. The fellow would give himself away in a minute. Irving sat down.

His visitor said abruptly, "You've heard of Santa's ledger account—his record of all the good and bad things people do?"

"I thought that was just for the children," Irving said. "If you've kept account of the Big Five and a Half, the debit side of your ledger must be full."

The blue cockatoo gave a raucous squawk and jabbed a hard beak against the bars.

"Overfull." Santa straightened, his pillow-stuffed stomach curving out like the back of a very large cat. "So it's time to close the accounts."

Irving looked up quickly at the jolly Santa Claus face that never changed. The voice, so maddeningly familiar, that came from behind the mask had an inhumanly detached sound.

Santa walked toward the bulging sack he had left in Irving's favorite chair and untied the heavy twine at its mouth. He took out a toy xylophone and laid it on the three thousand-dollar desk beside his host. "I'd like to leave this for your son, with the compliments of the season. And this is for your daughter." He set down a doll by the xylophone, fumbled for a moment in the sack, and brought out a book. "Here's something more for Irving Junior; I'm sorry for the kid. And as for Irving Senior, just for old time's sake…"

He brought out a flat box of chocolate-covered cherries.

"Cherry Snorts!" Irving's hand instinctively went out toward the box. *Better look out, Irv, or you won't be able to get close enough to a patient to fill a tooth.* His hand dropped. "No thanks, Santa. I'm putting on weight."

"Oh, come on, Irv. Just one. This is Christmas."

Irving's hand came out again and made its selection. Into his mouth went the brown, juicy morsel—and the poison inside it.

The Santa Claus figure waited. It was a quick-acting poison, and it wasn't long before his victim had stopped writhing on the great rug that had been a bargain at fifteen thousand dollars,

34

and Santa Claus was able to shoulder his pack and start out again.

Chapter Two

In the white living room of the penthouse, Mercy's two concessions to Christmas were multiplied on the mirror-lined walls. The coffee table, with its complication of holly, pine boughs, bright Christmas ornaments, and one thick red candle, became a hundred spots of color as mirror reflected mirror. The second concession, a clump of mistletoe as big and round as a basketball, swaying from a hook in the ceiling, became a hundred balls of gray-green.

The customers of Mercy Marsh, Inc. (she always thought of it as "Ink") liked to think that Christmas meant something—both to her and to them—that wasn't commercial, and it was her most important customers who knew where to find her away from the shop.

From the white divan, Mercy cocked her head at the nearest glass, one eyebrow up, one mouth corner deepening. How lucky it was that any habitual gesture should be so becoming. Of course, she would have changed it long before now if it hadn't been becoming. It was just a matter of fixing your conscious mind on it long enough to establish it in the unconscious. That was what she had always told Brooks about those silly habits he'd developed to hide his hands. But Brooks didn't have what it took to break himself of a habit. All he had was what the

Chandlers had given him, literally in money and intangibly in outlook and attitudes. It was too bad the money was going. At least the part that had gone into Mercy Marsh, Ink had thrived and multiplied. Though of course, it was no longer Chandler money; she'd been smart enough to see to that right from the start.

She got up off the low divan, watching the multiple Mercys rise. Not many women could bring themselves up so gracefully. Not many women could bring themselves up to her position in life as she had either. And few enough men.

"Most Likely to Succeed"She didn't know whether it was the smell of pine or the approaching dinner the caterers would prepare this afternoon that brought Mariposa back so clearly this morning. Mariposa and the Big Five and a Half. Well, the Half had made good. And so had two of the Five. She and Drew and Irving were well on the way to their first million.

Mercy stepped close to a mirror panel. Yes, she looked like a success—and she hadn't sacrificed her femininity to do it. The shining black hair, cut with Oriental bangs, the black-lashed, translucent gray eyes, the pixie face, the nearly virginal figure...yet she'd come up almost to the top in a world of male competition. Mercy Marsh, Ink, was already a leader among western dress designers, and someday she'd conquer the east...

And she'd done it all herself—with, of course, a start from the Chandler money. But it had been her brains and her skill and her management. You had to have money to get places fast, and Mercy couldn't see herself waiting until middle age for success. Brooks would have lost the money anyhow. So here she was—her peacock-blue lounging pajamas a rod of electric flame in the white, mirrored room—Mercy Marsh, of Mercy Marsh, Ink. A successful woman.

She turned sideways, eyes critical. Better watch the candy and drinks that went with the holiday season. Little curves were right for little girls, but it was sometimes hard to remember that growth went in two directions.

From the kitchen came the first notes of the chimes that meant someone had come up in the elevator. Half the time the downstairs door was unlatched, and her maid wasn't in on holidays. Mercy unlocked the elevator door that opened into the hall of the penthouse. Success would never leave her impervious to bells; either telephone or doorbell might mean business.

"Why, Santa Claus!" With a gesture that was almost involuntary, she pulled the door wide open.

A figure in a traditional Santa Claus costume stepped into the room on the great white rug. On his back, he carried the traditional Santa Claus pack. A customer from the store who found playing the role amusing...

Mercy gave him a welcoming smile. "It's been a long time since I've had a visit from Santa Claus. Or have you rung the wrong doorbell? I'm Mercy Marsh, of Mercy Marsh, Ink."

The Santa Claus figure stood facing her. The blue eyes behind his mask looked as old as his beard. "You don't need to tell me who you are, Mercy. You haven't changed."

She laughed—a high, thin, tinkle of Chinese wind bells made of glass touching glass.

"And your laugh hasn't changed. Or your voice."

"Santa Claus always did know everything about every child," she said. "Is he keeping track of the big children now?" The high, quick voice mocked him lightly.

"Only some of them," Santa said. "A chosen few. Wouldn't you expect to be among the chosen?"

Mercy laughed again. "Can it be that Santa Claus has turned acid? Or has my point of view changed?"

"I doubt if it's changed," Santa said. He made a sweeping gesture with one red-mittened hand. "Not with all these mirrors—and Mercy Marsh in the center."

"Self-centered," she murmured appreciatively. "I must say you're the most refreshing Santa Claus it's been my pleasure to meet."

"We aim to please our customers," Santa said. "You ought to know that, Mercy Marsh, of Mercy Marsh, Ink…. And speaking of wares…." He set down his pack on the corner of the low, white divan. "Do you mind if I rest my poor old back for a minute?"

"Not at all," Mercy said. "You ought to get that much out of Christmas. May I bring you a cup of Christmas cheer?"

"No thanks; you can't drink through these things." He touched his manufactured face with one mitten.

"Why not take it off?" Mercy asked.

"You might not like me anymore," Santa said.

"Don't children always like Santa?"

"Not when he leaves sticks and ashes in their stockings," Santa said.

"But sticks and ashes are for the bad children, Santa."

"Well?"

Mercy stood looking at him, her head tipped sideways, one eyebrow raised in speculation. The half-familiar voice, the eyes that might be those of someone she knew—or had known long ago.

"How long have we known each other, Santa Claus?" Mercy asked.

"Since you were born."

"Turn around, Santa."

The motion of his turning brought a whiff of pine to her nostrils. She pulled a branch out of the arrangement on the coffee table and waved it toward the red-suited man. "What does this remind you of, Santa Claus?"

He didn't say "Pine."

He said "Mariposa."

Mercy gave an audible sigh. "I thought so," she said softly. "But it didn't seem possible."

"What are you talking about?" Santa asked.

"Double talk is no special privilege of Santa Claus," Mercy said. "Like touring the world on Christmas Eve and going up and down chimneys. We ordinary mortals can use it too."

In the white, pine-scented room with its myriad reflections, Mercy's unmasked face showed pixie triumph. The other's expression was hidden behind the rosy, benign beam of Santa Claus.

He turned abruptly to his pack and began to untie the heavy twine that held it closed. "I have something here for you—"

"Sticks and ashes?" Mercy laughed.

"I'll give it to you and be on my way," Santa said. "I have several other places..."

Oh, no! This wasn't what she wanted.

"It's been so long..." Mercy began. "Don't go, Santa. Can't we talk for a while?"

Santa turned uncertainly, letting something slip back in his bag. "Was there something special—"

"Yes, there's something special," Mercy said. "Sit down, won't you, Santa Claus. I can't say it without any buildup."

"You're not the coy type, Mercy," Santa said. "Mercy—what a name for you."

40

"Dear Mister Claus—and I mean C-l-a-w-s," Mercy said. "If I were sensitive—"

Santa made an odd sound behind his mask.

Mercy laughed, sinking into a white chair as low as the divan.

"I'd never have gotten where I am if I'd been sensitive," she said. "Don't you think I've done well for myself, Santa Claus?"

"You've come a long way from Mariposa, if that's doing well for yourself," he said.

"Ask any well-dressed woman in San Francisco what Mercy Marsh, Ink stands for," Mercy said. "Ask Drew Lang. He handles my advertising. Ask Irving Pluit. His wife wears nothing but Mercy Marsh clothes—"

"Keep your shirt on, madam," Santa said. "That smart little shirt with the Mercy Marsh label. I didn't mean you hadn't done well for yourself financially."

"Well, for goodness sake, what other way—?"

Santa Claus held up a red-mittened hand.

"What about your own life?" he asked. "Where's the husband a young woman like you ought to have? Where're the children—"

Again, Mercy's laughter tinkled in the room.

The beaming face with the unsmiling eyes was steadily fixed in her direction. "There should have been a Chandler heir..."

She hoped the smile she gave him was natural. "But there wasn't, you see."

"Thanks to you and a certain doctor who shall at the moment remain nameless," Santa said. "After all, this is Christmas. I'll just whisper his address."

He leaned closer.

Mercy's fingers gripped the edge of her chair. "But I didn't give him my right name."

"Surely, my dear, you're not so naïve as to think you were

41

the only one who suspected you were pregnant—when you and Brooks were living on the same block as the Pluits and the Delorms!" Santa said.

Mercy shrugged. "Edith Pluit, I'll bet. She doesn't have enough to do. That type never does understand how a woman in business can't take time out for children—not and get anywhere."

"Most men don't understand it either, Mercy Marsh."

"I'd never have expected such a sentimental remark from you, Mister Claus," Mercy said. "Or are you just trying to stay in character, the character assumed with your suit?"

"I was thinking of Brooks," Santa said. "You deprived him of his only opportunity to be a father."

"Since when has thirty-one been past the age of virility?" Mercy asked. "He can marry again. And since when have you developed this sentimental outlook?"

"Santa Claus, you know, is sentiment itself."

"Then I hope the next time you come, you'll be wearing some other kind of suit. Superman or Hopalong Cassidy or—"

"But today's Santa's day, and I'm Santa," Santa said. "Before I give you what I have for you here—" He touched the bag. "—I'm going to point out your shortcomings."

Mercy drew up her knees and clasped her hands around them. "Do you think you have time, Santa dear? If you're going other places—"

"Not until I'm through with you, Mercy Marsh—completely through with you," Santa said.

"Dear Santa, if you didn't have that sweet, kind face, I'd say those words sounded sinister."

"Would you really?" he asked.

"So where are you going to begin, Santa Claus, way back in

Mariposa?" Mercy asked.

"It would take too long, Mercy Marsh," Santa said. "But of course that's where it began—even before you found you needed money to supplement your skill and personality in starting your own shop. And what was more natural when you thought of money than to remember the Chandlers, who'd always stood for money in the town where you'd grown up? Brooks was crazy about you."

"The next time you come no doubt you'll be wearing a Dick Tracy suit," Mercy said. "Your deductions are marvelous, Master Mind. So I married Brooks for the purpose of creating Mercy Marsh, Ink, instead of Chandler heirs."

"But Brooks didn't even get himself a business out of marrying you, in spite of the money he put into Mercy Marsh, Ink," Santa said.

"Why should I let him spoil it for me?" Mercy asked. "Brooks inherited his business ideas along with what was left of the Chandler money, made two generations ago—out of mining! You knew, didn't you, there wasn't half as much as all Mariposa had been thinking? And inheritance tax cut into that when his mother died."

"He might have been a success in one of the professions…" Santa asked.

"If there wasn't the slightest bit of competition," Mercy said. "Did you know he wanted to be a dentist? He had some wild idea of going in with Irving…"

"I suppose you know he lent Irving money to go to dental college, though he couldn't get in himself," Santa said. "But I'll bet you never thought—since you never think of anybody but yourself, Mercy Marsh—how it must have made Brooks feel to see Irving's success—and hear about it. Irv's not the modest-violet type."

"Why, that rug cost me five thousand dollars," she mimicked. "Is all this sympathy for Brooks just because it's Christmas, Santa Claus? Or are you trying to make me sorry for my past misdeeds?"

"Mercy Marsh sorry for anything that got her where she is today?" Santa said. "I know when I'm licked."

She laughed, the hands that had been clasped about her knees settling around each ankle. "You'd really have had something to say if I'd married Irving, wouldn't you?"

"He didn't have any money then, like Brooks," Santa said.

"Who's being naïve now, darling?" Mercy asked. "I didn't mean when I was starting Mercy Marsh, Ink. It was after Brooks had refused to put in any more, and I wanted to expand... but then I got some more big accounts and didn't have to worry."

"You and Brooks were still married?" Santa asked.

"Yes, dear; and so were Irving and Edith," Mercy said. "But there is such a thing as divorce, you know, and I was planning to divorce Brooks anyway."

"Of course you wouldn't have cared about a little thing like breaking up a family with two children," Santa said.

Mercy laughed again. "Not if they stood in the way of my business—as I believe you've pointed out. Besides, I'd have done those kids a favor to get them out from under Irving's thumb."

"Why didn't you try Drew Lang if you wanted to marry more money?" Santa asked.

Mercy cocked her head at him. "I thought of it, all right. But my feminine charms completely failed. Of course, he was brought up to shun women. Grandma Lang wouldn't let him go to dances or even movies for fear he'd be led astray. I guess it takes a Glenna to dent that man's armor—I almost said scales, meaning the kind that come on fish."

"Drew's never been what you'd call the warm type, I agree," Santa said.

"I must say I was surprised that even Glenna could land him," Mercy said. "I'd always expect him to be the fish that got away. It seems odd when he's so attractive. They say his mother was too."

"I saw a picture of her once that reminded me of Glenna," Santa said. "Not that it looked like her, just something about it... but getting back to this generation, Mercy, did you know that Red Delorm has been let out? Just this morning, for good behavior."

"But it hasn't been nine years," Mercy said. "It can't be more than two."

"You ought to know, Mercy Marsh; you played a bigger part in sending him up than Drew, who lost more money through him," Santa said.

"I did?" she asked. "Why, you're crazy. I never—"

"You knew Red's salary didn't run to Mercy Marsh clothes, even though he kept accounts for both you and Drew. But you kept egging Glenna on to buy, and then wouldn't give her more credit. You—"

"All right, all right." Mercy held up, palm out, both pink claw hands. "So now little Mercy, besides wrecking the life and fortunes of her own husband, made Glenna's husband commit the crime that put him behind bars."

Back of the white-whiskered outer lips, the lips that moved said, "Well?"

"Honestly, dear Mister Claus..." Mercy began.

"With a beautiful wife nagging for expensive clothes—a gorgeous gal who'd have no trouble getting them from other men—wouldn't you embezzle to give them to her? But, no, of course you wouldn't. You wouldn't care enough for anyone to understand it."

Mercy sat with upturned face, her oddly light eyes searching his, behind the Santa Claus mask. "Oh, wouldn't I, Santa dear?"

"And on top of all you did to Brooks and Red and planned on doing to the Pluits, when your old high school teacher—the one who's almost as responsible for your success as you are, Mercy, when he gave your name as a reference for a job that meant everything to him, at his age, in prestige and money both, what did you do but—"

"But nothing!" Mercy said. "I wrote a regular eulogy. On a reference like that and the things I said when they called me, a man could run for President."

"Pardon me if I raise an eyebrow, Mercy," Santa said. "Can you imagine any one of his references—all old and shall we say dear friends of Northcliffe—admitting to being the one who queered his chances?"

"You have a suspicious nature, don't you, Mister Claus?" Mercy said. "You know, it was smart of you to come incognito; we can say so many things that we couldn't otherwise. Now you've broken the ice…" Hands clutching ankles, Mercy rocked back and forth, moonstone eyes bright. "I'm a hard, scheming woman, you say. You'd be surprised if you knew the scheme I have now."

"Don't tell it to me," Santa said. "I don't want to hear another of your schemes. Just let me congratulate you on your business acumen in getting rid of liabilities like Brooks and Red and Northcliffe, and acquiring an asset like Glenna Lang, with the purchasing power of her present husband."

"I'm pleased, of course, about Glenna—" Mercy began.

"'Most Likely to Succeed'—you and Irving Pluit and Brooks Chandler and Drew Lang and Wally Fleming and Red Delorm…"

"Glenna should have been included, Santa," Mercy said. "I could have told you, even in high school, that she'd go farther than Brooks or Red."

"Don't all those names remind you of anything, Mercy?"

"Indeed they do," Mercy said. "They're all coming to dinner tonight. All except Red—I hope. What a reunion it would be if he came."

Behind his mask, the other's breath came audibly. But he didn't speak.

"Is it my turn now, Santa, to get in my two bits?" Mercy asked. "I can't wait much longer."

"For once I agree with you, Mercy."

She mustn't forget he liked people brittle and flip. Lucky thing, for by now she probably couldn't be anything else. "I'll get right to the point then, Santa—to that something special I thought I needed a build-up to say. Well, I haven't had quite the build-up I planned, but I guess it's now or never. You said I married Brooks for his money, and of course, you were right. And I told you I was willing to marry Drew or even Irving when I needed more money. Well, I don't need any more money now; Mercy Marsh, Ink, is more successful than I ever dreamed it could be."

She paused, and the man laid his red-mittened hand on the mouth of the sack beside him.

"But you were wrong about one thing, Santa Claus," she added. She got up and walked to the window. "You said I wouldn't ever want anyone as Red wanted Glenna. Well, maybe I wouldn't, in quite the same way. But I'd like to have a good husband, one who wouldn't be too demanding. He'd be useful in lots of ways. Since I don't have to marry for money again, I can marry for love."

Santa gave a muffled snort. "And what do you know about love, Mercy Marsh?"

"Enough to know I'd want marriage with it," she said. "I'm not Glenna's type."

"You're not as honest as Glenna," Santa said.

"If that's your idea of honest—"

"I didn't say—"

"Let's not quibble, my dear. Can't you see what I'm talking about? You never used to be obtuse. I've always admired your mind. Don't you know there's only one man I'd like to live with?"

"I don't suppose you'd care to tell me who you think you're talking to?"

Did he actually think he'd fooled her by running through that bag of tricks with his hands? First he'd stood with them behind him, the way Brooks stood so much; then he'd made a pointed roof of his mittens. You could tell every finger was pressed together inside, in the well-known gesture of the Big Five and a Half's special mentor and friend. A minute ago he'd even drummed with his fingers, like Red. She had seen them moving under the cloth of the mittens and heard the faint sound of each top. But he hadn't fooled her for a second.

Mercy came back from the window. "Do I need to tell you who I *know* I'm talking to—Cecil?"

Inside his padded red suit, Santa gave a visible start. "Look, Mercy—"

"Perhaps I should have waited," she said. "I'll go back to calling you Santa if that makes things easier. But I knew you'd never say anything to me until I made it plain that I wanted you to."

"Mercy, listen—"

"Okay, Santa," she said. "I've had my say. And we'll pretend I never said a word when you come back with a different face, now you know how welcome you are. Come early tonight. Let's get some benefit from the mistletoe besides decoration."

"Mistletoe!" The word fairly shot through the Santa Claus mask. "If that's not typical of a—of the tease—liar—cheat that you are, Mercy Marsh! You lead a man on with your graceful ways, and your pretty face, with your head on one side—and your bird-claw hands waiting to grab and tear—like any other claws."

"Why—why, Cecil! I mean Santa. What—"

"A lure! A decoy!" Santa said.

"Listen, Santa," Mercy said. "This is Christmas."

He stood looking at her, eyes gleaming behind the smiling mask. "You don't even know the truth when you meet it. There's no honesty in you."

"But there's a lot of success, dear Santa," Mercy said. "And success has its uses. Ask any one of the Big Five and a Half—any of those 'Most Likely to Succeed.' Ask Mister Northcliffe."

"I had my answer long ago," Santa said. "Now I'm going to give you yours." He reached for the mouth of the sack again. His mittened hands fumbled.

A purple donkey with long, floppy ears fell out onto the white divan.

Mercy clapped her little claw hands. "Oh, Santy. Presents."

He straightened and turned toward her with a box in his hand.

"Darling! Cherry Snorts!" she said. "And here I have to think about my figure. You know Mercy Marsh, Ink—"

"Yes, I know Mercy Mark, Ink," Santa said. "But I'll promise you something. One piece of this candy won't make you fat."

"Non-calorie candy?" Mercy said. "You think of everything, darling. I'll take this one then, next to the empty space."

In it went. Into the round, red "O" of her pixie mouth.

This time the Santa Claus figure didn't wait. He picked up his pack, thrust the purple donkey into it, and stumbled to the elevator while the body in the peacock pajamas still writhed on the thick white rug.

Chapter Three

She was calling again. Might as well get it over. There'd be no peace until he did. There mustn't be a repetition of that Sunday she'd pounded and pounded on his door and at last begun to whisper like an animal. She was an animal, of course—like his mother...

Drew turned the knob and stepped in quickly to get it over with.

As usual, the smell of her and her belongings and the heavy perfume she wore rose up like something tangible. It hit him with the same hard impact as the sight of her in the welter of flowers and satin hangings that made up her lair. No doubt she thought of it as a nuptial bower...

"You wanted to consult me?" he asked crisply.

She was standing by the bed—he always thought of her as she, not as Glenna, or as his wife—in a dull gold peignoir, with her back to him, the gold carried up to the top of her head by the glints in her hair. As usual, it was loose, gold-tinted, softly curling brown about her tanned shoulders. Someone must have told her what a beautiful back she had. Or she was building up to the climax of turning her face. She was an artist, really, in her way. Unless you preferred to call that sort of thing the tricks of her trade. No need to dignify it.

He waited at the door. If only she wouldn't touch him. He fixed his eyes on a great tub of giant poinsettias one of his clients had sent her for Christmas, but he couldn't keep them fixed.

Glenna was turning slowly away from the bed. Everything she did seemed to have a slow, deep rhythm that shook him. Perhaps just another trick of her trade, something she might have learned from Red or Brooks or Irving, or anyone else there might have been, like that lawyer fellow...

The side of her face was toward him now—the blunt, short nose, the full lips, the long-lashed eyes half-closed...

Three-quarter face, and pink lips parted in a lovely, slow smile. Had she schooled herself to smile, no matter what? Or was she just good-natured and kind? She'd been called "kind" on enough occasions... she and his mother.

She started toward him, and he drew himself in and upward, folding his arms.

Glenna laughed. She kept coming closer, her perfume stronger. "No wonder the kids used to call you Turtle. Remember, Drew?"

A foot away she stopped. "You're a handsome brute. You were even then. I've seen plenty of tow heads. But you—wow! And now, in a way, you don't look any older, just more distinguished and—expensive looking. Why, we were actually married before I found out your hair was really white. It was so nearly white before, it sort of sneaked up on you. Just think of not knowing the color of your husband's hair before you were married." She paused, still looking up, and her smiling face darkened with reproach. "If you call it married."

"Go down to City Hall and look at the records, Missus Lang—"

"You know that's not what I mean." She came a step closer

and laid her hand on one of his folded arms.

His muscles tightened. "You said you wanted to consult me."

Glenna sighed—a breast-heaving, pulse-quickening per-formance—and reluctantly removed her hand. "Didn't you say—come right out and say it, with all the romance in the world when you proposed—that there was no one you'd rather have at the end of the table from you, with all your prize clients in their best bibs and tuckers in between, than little old me?"

Drew laughed—that forced sound of mirth he reserved for clients, the only sounds of mirth he ever made. "There are some connoisseurs who would label little old you the finest piece of art in the house."

"Oh, you know your collectors' items, all right." Her husky voice was bitter. "I'll be a museum piece, too, before I know it. Who'd have ever thought it?"

"I didn't tell you—"

"That's right, Drew," Glenna said. "You told me you wanted a hostess when you entertained. And I was the only one you wanted—*wanted*! Excuse me while I smile. Oh, you told me what to expect, all right. What you didn't tell me was what *not* to expect."

"Don't forget the charge accounts at all the best stores, Glenna, and a checking account of your own, and having your beauty set off by one of the show places of San Francisco. Why, when I think of what a lot of women would give to be mistress of this house—"

"It's not the house I—"

"Let's not be vulgar, Glenna."

"If you don't sound like Grandma Lang!" she said. "If your dad was that way, I don't wonder your mother cleared out."

"We won't discuss my mother," Drew said grimly.

Glenna stiffened. Then suddenly her face softened, and the smile came back. "Aren't we just two old sillies, carrying on like this, when you're married to the best piece of art in your collection, and I'm married to the handsomest man I ever saw, my childhood sweetheart, you might say."

"I thought Red was your childhood sweetheart," Drew said. "You were both twenty when—"

"But honey, if you'd ever looked at me in those days, even just once, I never would have married Red. Don't you know—"

Her hand was coming out again, and Drew said quickly, "All right, Glenna, let's get this over with. I've got things to do."

"It's Christmas, Drew. Don't tell me you can't leave your nasty old business—oh, dear, I shouldn't call it nasty when it brought me that sweet little Cadillac this morning. But surely you can take enough time off on Christmas day to spend a few minutes with your wife, can't you?"

"Certainly, Glenna, if you'll tell me what you're worried about."

Glenna laughed softly. "Honey, that'd take me the rest of the day, and all night, and the next, and the next, and—"

"Look here, Glenna—"

She sighed again. "Okay, business first, last, and all the time. I wanted to ask you what to wear to the Pluits this afternoon. It'll have to be something I can go to Mercy's dinner in. Irving's only a dentist, and I thought he didn't advertise, but you said he owned the most stock in a couple of companies or something you do business with—"

"He's a highly influential client, my dear," Drew said. "As to what you wear... it's hard on the Edith Pluits of this world to have to entertain the Glenna Langs."

"Just what do you mean by that? I'm every bit as good—"

54

"It's according to your interpretation of the word, my dear," he said. "If you're thinking of your financial standing compared to hers, it's every bit as good, perhaps better since we got the Van Dyne account. Of course, if you're thinking of—oh, well, we won't go into that. Anything you wear will put poor Edith in the shade, and every other woman at the party. Just so it's not too low or otherwise indecent."

"Why would you care if it was—Mister Ice Water Lang?"

Drew suddenly found himself shaking. "My wife's not going to expose herself to every man who wants to look. She's not—"

"It'd be different," she flashed back, "if you wanted to keep me for yourself! If you cared two hoots—"

His crossed arms fell apart. One foot took the step that separated him from Glenna. Each hand closed on a round arm beneath the gold sleeves. "You're going to wear a decent dress! Hear me? No man's going to see any more of you than he's got a right to, again! Not while you're married to me."

Glenna's brown eyes brightened. "You're a dog in the manger, honey."

"What's further, I know what goes on when I'm not around," Drew said. "I've got a good private agency on the job."

The smile left her eyes. "Private agency! You don't mean—why, you dirty dog!"

Drew's hands dropped. "In the manger or out of it," he said with an effort of lightness. "I just wanted you to know."

"Thanks. Thanks a lot for your Christmas present."

He turned toward the door of the bathroom.

Glenna ran after him, her voice rising. "Now don't go wash your hands! I'm not poison!"

He hesitated, shaking.

"How do you think a girl feels when you go off to wash your

hands every time you touch her? Half the time all I need to do is look at you, and you run for soap and water. A jolly home life I got for myself!"

Poor kid, it was really tough. She wouldn't understand if he tried to explain, but he had to try. He owed her that much.

"I'm sorry, Glenna," he said. "It's not—just you. There's something in me… I can't explain it, but I've always been this way. You knew I had all those washbowls installed when I bought the house—long before you ever came here. Long before I ever thought you would. Glenna, it isn't you…"

"Drew, do you know what you just said?" Glenna said. She came closer, putting out her hand. Then she dropped it, while her dark eyes searched his face. "You said 'long before you ever thought I'd come here,' just like you wanted me to. Like you'd wanted me to for a long, long time."

He put both hands to his head and shut his eyes. "Glenna, don't."

"But, Drew dear, I think you love me. I think you really love me," Glenna said.

"Love—?"

"Poor Drew," Glenna said. "You don't know what love is. How could you, with Grandma Lang and your dad bringing you up?"

That hard, old hand and the stronger man's hand poised to strike… tongues to lash out at the mother who had gone, the mother Drew couldn't remember…

"They didn't have love to give you, Drew," Glenna said. "I could hardly eat your grandma's cookies, she seemed to hate me so."

Perhaps Gran had felt it too, this reasonless, deep certainty that this woman was his mother. But Glenna was just a young girl when she lived in Mariposa, and she'd married Red Delorm.

Gran couldn't have known the future. Besides he, Drew himself, was the one she always said was like his mother—looked like her, thought like her, and was bound to act like her.

"Glenna, I've got to wash. It isn't you. I've got to." He brushed past her to the bathroom.

When he returned, she was holding a dress against her body, a floaty, flame-colored thing, tucked under her chin. She tossed it on the bed and unzipped her gold gown. Drew hurried back into the bathroom and turned on the water again.

She came to the door. "You'll wear your hands out, Drew. Will you zip me up the back?"

She turned, a flame swirling, and presented a smooth back framed in a bright, waist-length V. He gritted his teeth and pulled the zipper.

"Goodness knows this one's modest enough, with a neck almost up to my ears in front. I don't know why I bought it, though. I'm not the flame-covered type."

"I should think—" Drew began.

"There's a big difference, darling, between being a flame and being flame-covered. Black's better on me. Unzip me, will you, honey?"

She was pulling it over her head before his hand had dropped. Eyes full of the sight of her in brief, black underthings, he reached blindly for the faucet.

"No, Drew!" She caught his hand. "If you can't get over that crazy notion by yourself, you must see a psychiatrist. I'll get the name of Edith Pluit's."

She pulled him through the bathroom door and kicked it shut.

"Glenna!" His voice was agonized. "Put something on."

"What a psychiatrist would say..."

Someone else to pry into him... to probe those deep recesses...

"For goodness sake, go look out the window or something," Glenna said. "Don't wash your hands again! A girl can take only so much."

"I'm sorry, Glenna," Drew said. "I wish I could make you understand." But how do you explain to someone something you don't understand yourself?

Go look out the window, she'd said. At least he could do that for her.

The window faced the front lawn. Now that the trees were bare, the street was just outside. He'd been wise to choose for himself a room at the back of the house. From here he could see two of those idiotic reindeer Glenna had wanted for Christmas decorations. Though only the holiday season and, on the balcony, the color of the suit on the object that passed for Santa Claus would make anyone think they were reindeer. Deer, sleigh, and Christmas saint were all just lumps in varying sizes, as if a child had made them from snow—in this land of no snow—adding at will pronged horns or a red suit and white beard. Abstractions, Glenna called them. Only the ladder to the Spanish balcony, sifted with artificial snow on rungs and railings all the way from Glenna's room in the front past his own in the back, showed plainly what it was—strong, solid wood built to hold the Irish handyman who'd put it up. He'd had a little trouble, Glenna said, getting the Santa Claus abstraction placed. She'd wanted it halfway up the ladder, but the lump's contours hadn't lent themselves to climbing, so she and the handyman had compromised on a foursquare position on the balcony at the top of the ladder as if it had just been scaled.

By leaning toward the corner of the house, Drew could see the Santa Claus lump. Perhaps it was the thing's stillness or its non-human shape that gave him a feeling of peace. He fixed his eyes on the red-suited object and leaned against the window frame.

But such peace couldn't last. Glenna was calling again.

He tensed himself and turned.

"I'm not going to wear this one, honey," she said. "So don't say what you're thinking. I had an idea, but it didn't come off. And the dress won't either; the zipper's caught. Can you help me, Drew? Don't look like you're headed for the gallows."

The smell of her in his nostrils again...teeth tight as the zipper he jerked at it.

"Take it easy, honey; that's my skin right underneath, you know."

He knew—knew with every inhalation, every motion of the satin body that, no matter how he strained away, was always there...

Glenna gave a throaty little chuckle and a wriggle. "This is almost like having a husband, Drew dear. One of the few domestic scenes these walls have ever witnessed. Don't you think it would be fun—?"

Another jerk, and he was free. And halfway to the bathroom.

But Glenna was before him. Flat against the door. "No, you don't, Drew Lang! Wash your hands once more and I'll go raving, tearing nuts!"

Groaning, he turned to the window where he had found a few minutes' respite. The skin on both hands was drawn, as if they had been in slime that was drying...slime of unspeakable filth...only soap and water...

He found the window frame again.

Outside, the two leaders and half the next pair of abstract reindeer stood lumplike on the lawn. If only he'd stayed at the office... but you didn't go to your office on Christmas Day. If he locked himself in his room now without helping Glenna decide what to wear, she'd be furious enough to go to the Pluits à la Lady Godiva. And there'd be Irving... and probably Brooks... under the pull of dried slime, Drew's hands began to burn.

He folded his arms, hands made into fists to let no slime touch his jacket. *Don't think of Glenna*, he told himself, *or of dirty hands. Concentrate on the reindeer...*

He leaned against the window frame to see it. Surely the thing was heavy enough or anchored well enough so the wind couldn't move it. Not that there was any wind; the trees were as still as the lumpish reindeer. But just a few minutes ago, before Glenna had called him, hadn't the Santa Claus lump been nearer the top of the ladder, facing the street more directly? He hadn't looked at it then with any thought of remembering; he had only a vague impression with which to compare the way it looked now. He couldn't say its position had actually changed, any more than he could say that the bare root or so of balcony railing on the other side of the ladder had had artificial snow on it then. His impression was that the snow had been unbroken as far as he could see the railing. But you couldn't depend on impressions. Ask any lawyer. Not that it mattered, as far as the fake Santa Claus and fake snow were concerned. Only that, by his change of preoccupation, when Glenna said, "All right, Drew. How's this?" he was able to turn around, able to keep all signs of emotion from his voice when he gave his approval.

There was something about the long-sleeved, black gown she had on that was faintly nun-like—until he took a second look. Trust Glenna to wear the kind of clothes that would make him—or any other man—take a second look. But at least it wasn't blatantly inviting.

"Will I be a credit to you now, Drew?"

"Shouldn't Mercy Marsh, Ink, get the credit?" he asked. He tried to speak lightly. "We advertisers—"

"Drew Lang!" she exploded. "Aren't you ever human?"

That awful dryness was pulling at his hands again.

"Please, Drew." She came closer, but at least she didn't touch him. "A woman doesn't have to be either a museum piece or a street-walker. She can just be a woman who wants a normal life."

The fists under his elbows trembled. "What's a normal life?"

"I don't know whether you're being sarcastic or whether you really don't know," Glenna said. "But I'll give you the benefit of the doubt, which is more than you've ever given me. A normal life, the way I see it..."

She came a step nearer, and then several steps in a rush. "It's having a home, and a husband who loves you, and children. It's—"

"What!"

"Yes, Drew, I said children. I've never felt that way before. But for you..."

Drew made a strange sound in his throat.

"I've always wanted to keep my figure and—that young look, whatever goes into making it. I never stopped to think until after we were married that losing my figure wouldn't have to be more than temporary, with good doctors and massage and diet, and that maybe having children—a little Drew and a little Glenna..."

His hands jerked free from his elbows.

She ran the few steps left between them and flung herself against him as if she thought he wanted her in his arms.

"Oh, Drew, we'd be so happy."

She caught his hands. "Here, Drew, put them here, in my hair. Now draw me close. Like this."

She was straining to bring his head down to hers when his fingers, tangled in her hair, began to close.

"Stop, Drew! You hurt. Not that way—you're pulling!"

"I've kept my promise," Drew said. "Emeralds and Cadillacs and—"

"Oh, yes, I've got—emeralds and—Cadillacs and—the name of Lang!" Her words came in jerks as his fingers tightened. "Talk about—the guy that—sold his—birthright—for a—mess of pottage. All I—sold mine for—what a mess!"

His hands loosened in her hair and moved to her throat. Not until the scream they cut off dropped to a gurgle did he release her and run for the door. Run down the hall. Slam his own door. Lock it. Lean against it, panting.

He'd never come so close to killing anyone. Poor Glenna... poor kid... he hadn't thought of it as Glenna in his hands. He hadn't thought at all. Everything he'd been standing for all his life had just gripped him suddenly, as he had gripped her. Until at last, just in time, some sense had returned.

His first motion away from the door had been to the washbowl. Then he sat down at his desk and let the monotone austerity of the rooms—walls, ceiling, rug, and the few bare furnishings blending into the monk's cloth at the balcony windows—soak into him. No perfume, no flowers, no clutter, no voice to pry...

It was several minutes before he noticed the open sheet of letter paper on the desk, another before his eyes focused on the two handprinted lines: "When you know that Santa Claus isn't a person but an abstract idea, then he's real."

Too bad he hadn't thought of that when he was little. No

child ever needed to believe in Santa more than he had. But the Santa Claus story had been for boys who had mothers.

Too tired to wonder how the paper had come to his desk, he sat there absorbing the message. An abstract idea... someone—was it Glenna when she set up those lumpy things on the lawn, or was it some modern artist?—said abstractions came nearer to the essence of things than the things themselves...

He didn't know when he became aware of a different smell in the room. He got up slowly and turned around.

A red-suited figure stood beside the open closet door that had been closed a few minutes earlier.

"Thank you, I accept with pleasure," the figure said.

"Accept what?" Drew asked simply.

"Your invitation to come in."

"I gave no invitation."

"Thinking of me was the invitation. I'm not a person, you know. I'm an abstract idea. You read my message?" He glanced toward the paper on the desk.

"I have you to thank for that?"

The figure nodded. "It's too bad we don't understand such things when we need them most."

"And that is—?"

"When we're children. A visit from Santa Claus would have meant a lot to young Drew Lang in Mariposa."

"Did you come up the ladder out in front?" Drew asked abruptly.

The other nodded again. "That's one of the nice things about Christmas; I always know I'm welcome."

"I told her she was asking for trouble," Drew said. "In broad daylight, too..."

The Santa Claus figure set his bulging bag on the desk. "Don't you want to know what I've brought you?"

Drew said slowly, "There's only one thing I want for Christmas—or any other time—and it doesn't come in a Santa Claus pack."

"Have you forgotten the Letters-to-Santa-Claus Department, Drew?"

"Let's quit our kidding, Santa Claus. Is it money you want, or Missus Lang's jewels, or my art treasures?"

"My dear Drew, I'm sure you don't often make such errors in judgment or your business wouldn't be what it is. I've come to bring you the gift you want most."

Taller and broader than the Santa Claus figure, Drew Lang stood looking at him. "Let's see it," he said.

The red mittens fumbled with the cord at the neck of the bag and brought out a flat cardboard box.

Drew's face lit up. "Cherry Snorts!"

Santa Claus took off the lid and held out the box.

The other's hand came out and paused. "Who got the other two?"

"Two of those 'Most Likely to Succeed.' Santa's reminding all the Big Five and a Half of the happiest days of their lives."

Drew took the piece in the farthest corner. Put the chocolate marble into his mouth...

Santa Claus waited for only the few minutes he needed to be sure before he took the note off the desk, picked up his pack, and walked around the balcony to the ladder.

Chapter Four

I n front of the fire in the chintz-covered wing chair that balanced the worn leather monstrosity where her husband sat, Adrienne Fleming tossed the last of the scrambled Christmas wrappings into the flames and drew her feet up, smiling at Wally.

Behind him, a tree as high as the ceiling, with ornaments of all periods and colors, lighted with every shade of bulb, filled the corner of the room, while dolls, bats, balls, ties, books, games, and phonograph records littered every usable surface.

Another wonderful Christmas, Adrienne thought, in a wonderful series, with Wally the world's nicest husband, and the girls and the twins the nicest children.

"Ten years and four children, and you're still the little blonde with dimples I first fell for," Wally said proudly.

"And you're still—everything you should be, Wally dear, only more so," Adrienne said.

Wally leaned his head against the leather chair back. "Smells like Christmas used to in Mariposa, honey. Turkey… onions… plum pudding… spruce… I swear you can even smell last night's bayberry candles. I'm glad I married you, Missus F., as you may have gathered."

Adrienne's dimples came out again. "I endorse that statement in reverse, Mister F.—even if one of the fruits of our marriage does have to have her teeth straightened. It's going to shoot our budget higher than Ursa Major."

"One of the things I like about you is the way you adjust to being an astronomer's wife, even—"

"I don't know how we'd get along if I didn't."

"Even if, as I started to say before I was rudely interrupted, you should have said—"

"Don't tell me I should have said Ursa Minor because it's a million light-years farther from the earth or something," Adrienne said. "And don't tell me that's wrong, either. What's another million light-years in the span of one human life?"

"Not a tenth of one percent in yours, my love, I know. That's why I appreciate your efforts."

"You know what's important to you is important to me, Wally, whether my intellect's up to grasping it or not."

She jumped out of her chair and aimed a kiss at the top of his head. He caught her and pulled her down into his lap. They settled back together with her short yellow curls on his shoulder.

Against scratchy tweed that smelled like his pipe tobacco, she murmured, "You were so smart to set up the new train in the boys' room and give us all this peace and quiet to enjoy the Christmas smells. Though I really ought to baste the turkey and get the yams started."

His arms tightened. "Later, honey. Just think, if you'd married Irv Pluit, you'd have your kids' teeth straightened for free."

"It wouldn't have been worth it, Wally, because my kids wouldn't have been yours."

"Then you don't mind too much being married to a poor professor—an assistant professor at that—instead of a big money-maker who'll probably be several times a millionaire before he dies?"

They'd had this out too many times—the question of a service career versus making money—to rouse her to battle anymore. She only said, without even lifting her head from his shoulder, "Just take a look at Irving—and Drew—and Mercy. They're the biggest money-makers we know. Are they happy?"

"I'll never forget," Wally recalled, "how excited you were the day I met you—and you met Mister Northcliffe—about what was going to happen to us—all the Big Five and a Half—because of his continually pounding into us the need to make money."

Adrienne sat upright. "Well, take another look at Irv and Drew and Mercy! All the others hate them. Why, even Brooks and Mister Northcliffe hate you—you, of all people!—because they think you stood in the way of their making money. Brooks was going into partnership with Drew (as if Drew would take him!), and Mister Northcliffe from landing that fat committee job he was angling for. And Brooks told me that Red hates you too on account of Glenna. That lawyer you took the trouble to get for him at the time of his trial… it seems Glenna—"

"So I heard," Wally said. "Poor Red, you can't blame him."

"But it wasn't your fault! Anyway, look at your Big Five and a Half—hating or being hated or both, with Brooks and Mister Northcliffe as bitter as they come, and Red Delorm in the penitentiary. All because of money! Was I right or wasn't I about Mister Northcliffe's teachings?"

"My dear, I wouldn't dream of saying you weren't right about anything, except maybe in my own special astronomical province. A man has to preserve some rights, you know, in these days of growing female dominance."

"Even Glenna was tainted," she rushed on, "without being

one of his favorite pupils… you know, darling, I didn't at all mind naming the twins Brooks and Drew when you suggested it. I know what it must have meant to those lonely men. But if you'd wanted to name one of the girls Glenna, I think I'd have just about died."

Wally laughed and kissed her. "You don't need to be jealous, honey. I've never been one of Glenna's men."

"But if you had planned to name one of your daughters Glenna, I'd have been sure you wanted to be."

As his arms closed around her, the doorbell rang.

"Don't worry, my love, when we have our next girl. As far as I'm concerned, you're a howling success." He kissed her again and set her on her feet.

"That joke had whiskers on it," she said severely, on her way to the hall, "even when my name was Howell."

It took her only a minute to go to the door and return. "Here's something else with whiskers, dear—the kid we all welcome at Christmas." She stepped aside to allow a figure dressed in a Santa Claus suit to come in. "You entertain him, Wally, while I get the children."

"Don't get them yet." The figure's voice was muffled by his mask. "I'd like to rest a minute, if I may."

Adrienne laughed and sat down, waving the Santa Claus figure to a chair. "Poor man! When I think of what our four can do to us…"

"And the numbers he's probably coped with this morning," Wally added.

The red-suited figure, making no move toward the chair, sighed behind his mask. "Yes, Santa's tired. It's been the biggest Christmas I've ever had. I'd like to give you what I bought you, though, before I settle down." He was fumbling, without taking off his mittens, at the string trying up his bulging sack.

Adrienne stood up. "I hate to have the children miss this. Do you mind if I call them?"

The rosy mask shook negatively. "This box is for adults only."

"Oh, not candy! Not even Cherry Snorts." Adrienne had seen the box as he drew it out. "We made a solemn pact with the children to eat no more than one piece of candy a day during the holiday season, and we all had our piece at the tree."

"But this is very special," Santa said. "He had the cover off now and was holding out the box—toward his host instead of his hostess.

Each of the remaining brown balls of chocolate gleamed in the Christmas tree lights.

Wally's hand had begun to leave the arm of his chair, and Adrienne started for the kitchen. It wasn't fair to make an issue of their promise to the children when chocolate cherries with brandy in them meant what they did to that little group of once-close friends from Mariposa.

"If you two'll excuse me, I have to baste the turkey... I'll bring back some wine," she called over her shoulder. If her husband was going to backslide, she wouldn't embarrass him by watching.

The box in Santa Claus' hand was only an inch from Wally's. "Just one," urged the voice behind the mask. "You'll have plenty of time to eat it before she gets back."

Wally's hand dropped to the chair arm. "When a fellow's lucky enough to have a wife like that, he's a fool to take any chances, even little ones. Thanks just the same. Sit down and we'll have a glass of wine when Adrienne comes back, and maybe after that, you'll feel like tackling the kids."

"You sure you won't...?" The candy came closer.

"I'm sure. Thanks again. Would you care for some Christmas music, Santa?" Wally leaned toward the radio.

"Spare me. I've heard enough Christmas hot air, including carols, to fill a balloon."

Wally laughed. "Shades of the Santa Claus tradition! Though I don't know how long you're expected to live up to it. Until you take off your suit, I suppose. Is this the last house on your beat?"

"The very last... when I leave here I'll never wear this suit again."

"You speak as if you were going to burn it."

"I am."

He laid down the box of cherries on the table by Wally's chair and began to rummage in his overstuffed bag. Three ties—green, blue, and red, fantastically painted—dangled over the edge of the table below the open box.

For a moment, the room was filled only with Christmas aroma, sluggish pops from the somnolent fire, and the quest of mittened hands in Santa's pack.

A child's voice calling from upstairs came in clearly. "Brooks has blood on him, Mama. All over his face. He can't see at all."

Wally almost collided with Adrienne coming in the door with a wine bottle and three glasses on a tray. She set them down and ran after him.

The tempo of his rummaging increased.

"Looking for something, Santa Claus?"

The red-suited figure whirled—to see his counterpart in the doorway. A second Santa Claus in a red suit, black boots, red mittens, red stocking cap, and a white-bearded mask stood looking in. He, too, held a bulging brown bag.

"Better try somewhere else," said the first Santa Claus. "I've got this territory covered."

The second Santa was looking about the big lived-in room with the Christmas tree in one corner. "I take it you haven't yet seen the man of the house?"

"He and the Missus have gone to render first aid to their offspring."

"Accounting for the three empty glasses, of course." The other held one toward the light. "Not used yet, I see."

"Aren't you smart, Brother Claus? Christmas morning's almost over if you're going someplace else…"

Behind his mask, the second Santa groaned. "I wish I had been smart."

The big room was now completely still. The sleepy fire lay dormant. The rat-like scrambling had ceased.

The first Santa Claus spoke again, standing with his hands behind his back. "Forgive the reminder, but, as I said, I've got this territory covered."

The second man's mask turned toward the antique mahogany-framed clock on the mantel, then back toward the other mask. "Have you heard the news lately?"

"What news?"

"It's time for it now; I've been watching. I heard it a while ago." He stepped to the radio, head bent toward the voice that came in softly. "Here we are… soon as he gets through with the U.N. squabble… and now that airplane disaster, and… here it is!" He turned up the volume.

"Another victim," came the voice of the announcer, "has been added to the list of violent deaths this bright Christmas morning. At ten o'clock the well-known dentist, Doctor Irving Pluit, major stockholder in more than one thriving Bay Area industry, was found dead on the floor of the study in his palatial new residence in the Park Merced district. Death was apparently caused by poison, although no autopsy report has yet been released. An hour later, the beautiful bride of the prominent advertising executive Drew Lang telephoned headquarters in a hysterical condition to say that when her husband failed to answer repeated knocks on the door of his combined bedroom-study at their artistic home in St. Francis Wood, housing treasures from all quarters of the globe, she ran along the outside balcony connecting their rooms and, through glass doors, saw him lying motionless on the floor. Upon breaking in, the police found him dead. The report of a third Christmas victim has just been released. This victim, a woman, found on the floor of her Nob Hill penthouse, is chic, attractive Miss Mercy Marsh, famed designer of women's clothes and accessories and head of the growing San Francisco firm of Mercy Marsh, Incorporated. An employee of the catering firm Johnson and Phailing arrived at the penthouse to begin preparations for a dinner Miss Marsh had planned for tonight. That dinner will never take place. When the buzzer, pressed at intervals for half an hour, failed to bring any response, the manager of the apartment house was summoned, and, after one glimpse inside, the police found Miss Marsh as described. All three deaths were apparently caused by poison. At three households this bright Christmas morning death has knocked on the door—death instead of Santa Claus. A more cheerful side of Christmas, however, may be observed—"

The man who had turned on the radio snapped it off. "Death instead of Santa Claus?" His voice rose in a question as his eyes met those of the other red-suited, white-whiskered masquerader.

The second arrival went on slowly. "You and I know something else the victims had in common. They were three of the six voted 'Most Likely to Succeed' in the Class of—"

"Never mind going through the routine," the other interrupted. His fingers began to drum inside his mittens on the table by Wally's chair.

For the space of three clock ticks the room was still.

The second Santa broke the silence. "It'll only be a matter of time before someone figures out the Mariposa connection and checks on the others. Just a matter of time—and maybe very little—before police ring Brooks Chandler's doorbell in San Francisco; and Red Delorm's, wherever his doorbell, or its equivalent, may be; and Wally Fleming's in Berkeley. They may be here any minute."

"And they may not," the first Santa Claus said. "That connection might not be made for days."

"But it will be made."

"Eventually, of course." Santa One seemed restless. He picked up his lumpy sack, carrying it with him as he circled the room, setting it down briefly before a tall pair of brass scales for weighing gold, standing on an oval table, and before the old clock on the mantel. At the scales, he changed the balance with a mittened hand. At the clock, he merely stood looking, red mitten tips and red thumbs pressed together, eyes recessed in the mask following the movement of the pendulum behind the Mount Vernon scene on the glass. Moving on to the table by the door where Adrienne had set the tray, he dropped his bag beside the other Santa's, and turned to face into the room.

With sharp blue eyes, Santa Two had been watching. He had taken off one mitten, and the hand released, oddly naked-looking, was pressed against his billowy stomach at the edge of his coat. "There are two things not hidden by disguises like ours," he said, "a man's height at the color of his eyes."

The other made a barking sound that might have been intended for laughter. "And how many men are there in the world about five-ten, with blue eyes?"

The second Santa countered, "How many among the Big Five and a Half answer that description?"

"So, out of the hundreds of thousands of people around the Bay, you pick out six!"

"Why were all three victims among those six? Why has Santa Claus come to the house of another member of that group?"

"If you know so much, you know the answers."

The second Santa sighed. "I guess I keep hoping there's some way to make it easy. When you've known someone as long as I have you..."

The other bent to pick up a bulging bag.

"That's my pack!" Santa Two's voice had a whip-like crack. "Set it down!"

The bag slid to the floor, Santa One's eyes on the automatic in the other's right hand.

With his left hand, still mittened, the second Santa Claus patted his well-rounded stomach. "There are other uses for this pillow besides making a paunch. You know I can't let you leave."

The eyes of the first Santa Claus were making a circuit of the room as his feet had just done. They came to rest on the chocolate cherries behind Wally's chair. Then they moved to the table near the door where Adrienne had set the wine and glasses.

The second Santa Claus spoke again. "There are only two in the Big Five and a Half who meet our description, as I've just pointed out. Unless you want to count their teacher."

"Why not?" A mask can cover an old face just as well as a young one, if you'd call thirty-something still young. And Northcliffe would have as much reason as any." He bent over the sack nearest him—his own, this time—and fumbled inside with his hands, his back half turned toward the other man.

"As much as any," Santa Two agreed. "And you could fill those bags with reasons for Red Delorm and Brooks Chandler and Mister Northcliffe to hate the ones who've succeeded."

Santa One made no reply. The only sounds in the room were the ticking of the clock and his moving hands.

"You know those reasons as well as I do," Santa Two said to Santa One. "There's no use going into them now... are you hunting for something, Santa Claus?"

The figure bending over the sack didn't turn. "Just repacking my bag a bit. The corner of a jumping-jack box or a toy piano digs into me every place I put it." As he spoke, he stopped his rummaging and partially straightened. But his hands, behind his back from Santa Two, were still busy. "Adrienne always said success meant too much to the Big Five and a Half. She was right, of course. We all know it now."

"We all know it now," Santa Two echoed. His voice was infinitely sad.

Santa One turned around, his hands still at last. Both bags stood in their respective positions on the floor as they had been, the bottle and three wine glasses in their positions on the tray. He gave another of those barking laughs. "Let's drink to Adrienne—the little blonde who was right—in the Fleming's own sherry. It's never been opened, I see."

He uncorked the bottle and, half turning his back again, poured wine into two of the glasses. Holding out one, he came toward the second Santa Claus. His big red mittens covered

75

the stem and most of the contents of both.

Santa Two shook his head. "Not with your sack of toys that near the tray. Even if the bottle was still sealed, the glasses weren't. I'd like to have a look in that sack of yours."

He pulled back the edge of the bulging bag in which Santa One had been hunting and peered in.

A stealthy movement made him raise his head.

Santa One was going through the doorway with both full glasses.

Santa Two caught him at the foot of the stairs. The automatic jabbed into back ribs where there was no pillow.

"Well, it was worth a try," the first Santa sighed as he set the glasses back on the tray in the living room.

"Gee," said a very young voice behind them, "two Sanna Clauses!"

Both Santas whirled.

A boy of four or five stood in the doorway. He had Adrienne's yellow curls and Wally's black eyes. Against the curls was a patch of fresh gauze and adhesive tape. "Mama said I could come down and see what I found in the living room. I never thought—gosh, I'm going up to tell her!"

As the child faced about, the first Santa caught him, and the other's gun dug into his ribs again.

"Don't tell the kids about seeing us," Santa One whispered into his small ear. "It's our secret, just yours and ours—and Daddy's. You can take him this glass of wine and tell him it's from Santa Claus."

He reached for one of the glasses he had just set down—the one Santa Two had refused.

The gun pushed harder against Santa One's ribs, who gave his barking laugh. "You know you wouldn't do it in front of the kid, Brother Claus. And I know it too… take it up to Daddy," he said again, closing the small, outstretched hand around the stem of the glass.

The little boy started off with short, tight-rope steps. Daddy's wine mustn't spill, his gift from Santa Claus. But his unflagging, four-year-old interest was caught by the open box of candy cherries by his father's chair. He paused.

The gun left Santa One's ribs as Santa Two clawed at his pack. Out came a box of chocolate cherries. He took off the lid. Every paper cup held its round, brown marble.

"Here," he said, "give me the glass, and take this up to your Dad. Have a piece yourself." He made the exchange and gave the small shoulders a push toward the stairs. The child broke into a short-legged trot.

Santa Two's hand went up to his brow. But you can't wipe sweat off a mask.

Santa One's voice came out harshly. "It's easy to replace missing pieces—or to bring any number of new boxes in that big sack of yours. I'd like to know where you were this morning—in your Merry Christmas disguise—when three people were poisoned? Three people who loved Cherry Snorts."

The two faced each other. Two identical suits, caps, and boots. Two identical masks. Merry Christmas disguises…

"I was home," Santa Two said firmly, "in what passes for home. And I can prove it."

"So was I, Brother Claus. That's my story too."

The tick of the clock came louder as the silence grew.

"There isn't much time," Santa Two said slowly. "I don't know when the police will get here, but it won't be long before Wally and Adrienne come down. You saw they'd bandaged the child."

"I don't suppose—"

The doorbell rang. A loud peal. Long. A finger still on the button.

Feet hurried down the stairs, and Adrienne's green dress fluttered past the door.

A man's heavy voice said, "I don't want to alarm you, Missus Fleming—"

Neither Santa heard the rest, for the one who had come to the Fleming house first picked up the glass of wine he had tried to give away. Tipped his mask. Thrust the glass under.

The sound of his fall was covered by the voice still booming in from outside.

The second Santa Claus stepped into the hall, a new stoop in his shoulders.

"There he is!" Two policemen burst through the door together.

As their hands fell on his red-clad arms, the Santa Claus figure said quickly, "Don't go in there, Adrienne. Wait just a minute. I'd like to tell you—"

"That's not the Santa Claus we were talking to!" Adrienne cried. "It's not the same voice."

"It's the other one you want, Officer," said the one whose arms were held. "I hoped he'd be gone before you saw me—like this, Adrienne." He glanced down at his pillow-stuffed suit. "I had the costume, with a full pack of toys and Cherry Snorts for tonight's reunion. So I put it on; I couldn't let him see my face and know I knew about him. I couldn't trample his pride any more. After all, he was taught... you know I wouldn't have let him get Wally, don't you?"

"So it's another Santa Claus we want, is it?" broke in the smaller policeman. "Anyone in a suit like this...don't think you weren't seen at the Pluits and Langs!"

The Santa Claus figure disregarded the policemen, his eyes still fixed on Adrienne. "You understand how it is, don't you? How it was. He couldn't go to the reunion tonight or let the others go, believing they'd all talk about him, ridicule him, gloat. And Christmas Day gave him the chance to wear a disguise bringing automatic welcome and turn the suspicion on a vengeful convict just released..."

"Convict!" Adrienne exclaimed. "What—?"

"Red Delorm. I went to see him in San Quentin, and he told me he'd be out Christmas morning, but he didn't want his other friends to know. I only told one because they were both so alone, but the one I told..." The Santa Claus figure sighed. "I guess he's ready now, Officer."

"They all learned the same lesson, but he took it most to heart. In there..."

By now Wally had appeared at the head of the stairs and came running down them. He stopped at the living room door. "Another Santa Claus!"

He and one policeman ran in.

The other stayed with the Santa in the hall, who said sadly to Adrienne, "I don't suppose I need to tell you it's Brooks Chandler they'll find," and to the officer who held him, "But I'm guilty too, for I taught him to need success. I didn't realize what I'd done until I came to San Francisco recently and saw my favorite students. I'm Cecil Northcliffe, and I taught them all."

A Note from the Author

Eunice Mays Boyd was my, Elizabeth Reed Aden's, godmother.

Slay Bells is set near Stonestown in San Francisco probably between 1960 and 1963. I have taken my clues from the geography and description of the homes. My mother rented a room from Eunice and her mother in the mid-1940s. They remained close friends up until Eunice's death in 1971. In 1960, my family moved to Ingleside Terrace in San Francisco. We could see Stonestown and 20th Avenue from our living room window and St. Francis Woods was less than half a mile away. The floors in our house, built in 1924, were Honduran mahogany. That is where the similarities end. My step-father was a physician—not a dentist.

When Eunice, or "Nana", died on February 4, 1971, she left me many things. Some jewelry, a framed *Pennsylvania Gazette* from 1758, and unpublished manuscripts. When the estate was settled and the articles in Nana's will were distributed I was in graduate school on the East Coast. My mother relieved me of the burdens of dealing with Nana's bequests and stored my inheritance safely at her house for decades.

At the time of Nana's death, she was working on a novel set primarily in Carcassonne, in the south of France. I read a draft of that novel in 1970, and she left me her working draft in a clipboard. I kept those hundreds of yellowed pages with me in a safe place for the next 40 years. In 2014, my husband Mel and I traveled to Europe, and I insisted we visit Carcassonne. After Mel returned to the States, I reread a scanned copy of her book set in the restored medieval walled city. I stayed at one of the hotels Nana mentioned and visited some of the places she described. I communed with her that day in April over croissants and café au lait.

When my mother died in 2016, I discovered three more of Eunice's unpublished novels in cardboard boxes while cleaning out my mother's house. Nana was very important to me, and a cornerstone figure in my life. I wanted to honor her by publishing her novels. I have made some necessary edits to modernize aspects of the work.

Eunice was born and raised in Oregon. She graduated from the University of California in 1924 after her family moved to Berkeley. She also spent twelve years living in Alaska. Her published books are: *Murder Breaks Trail* (1943), *Doom in the Midnight Sun* (1944), and *Murder Wears Mukluks* (1945). Among the unpublished novels *One Paw Was Red* is the fourth mystery also set in Alaska featuring her amateur detective, F. Millard Smyth. She was the "E" in Theo Durant, a group of authors, who each wrote a chapter in *The Marble Forest* (1950), which was made into the movie *Macabre* starring Jim Backus in 1958.

Acknowledgements

I want to thank the following people who have helped me bring Dune House to life. My editor, Jim Gratiot, for his patience and persistence. Laura Duffy took on the challenge of designing a series of covers for these Vintage Mysteries by Eunice Mays Boyd. I also want to acknowledge the very helpful guiding hand of Alan Rinzler who suggested republishing Eunice's earlier works. Special thanks also go to Eunice's nephew, Harry Watson Mays, and her grandnephews John and Kirk Rademaker, and their sister Erica for their support and permission to publish these novels.

About the Authors

Eunice Mays Boyd (1902-1971)

Eunice was an award-winning mystery writer during the Golden Age of Agatha Christie. Her books are intelligent, cozy whodunnit murder mysteries with many twists and turns. She loved to read mysteries and prided herself in identifying the murderer well before the end. After graduating from UC Berkeley in 1924, she moved to Alaska where she lived for 12 years. Circa 1940, she returned to Berkeley where she wrote the Alaska-based F. Millard Smyth mystery series: **MURDER BREAKS TRAIL** (1943), **DOOM IN THE MIDNIGHT SUN** (1943), and **MURDER WEARS MUKLUKS** (1945). These will be republished in 2022. A fourth book in the series, **ONE PAW WAS RED** will be forthcoming (2022/2023). She coauthored **THE MARBLE FOREST** that was made into the movie "Macabre" (1958). Her new cozy murder mysteries are: **DUNE HOUSE** (11/23/2021), **SLAY BELLS** (12/7/21) and **A VACATION TO KILL** FOR (2022). These books are published with her goddaughter, Elizabeth Reed Aden. **DUNE HOUSE** and **SLAY BELLS** are set in San Francisco, California, and **A VACATION TO KILL FOR** is set primarily in Carcassonne, France.

Elizabeth Reed Aden

Eunice inspired Elizabeth "Betsy", her goddaughter, to write her own medical thriller *The Goldilocks Genome* (2023), highlighting the importance and impact of personalized medicine. Betsy has a doctorate degree in anthropology. Her forthcoming book *HEPATITIS Beach* (2023/24) describes how a young woman's experiences living on a remote island in Melanesia where she studied the transmission of hepatitis B virus, changed the course of her life and career. She treasured and guarded the draft of *A VACATION TO DIE FOR* which she was given when

Eunice died. In 2017 she discovered three boxes containing *DUNE HOUSE*, *SLAY BELLS*, and *ONE PAW WAS RED*. Eunice was an important person in her life and she is proud that she is able to share Eunice's intelligent, cleverly constructed murder mysteries from the Golden Age.

SOCIAL MEDIA HANDLES:
 Facebook: Elizabeth Reed Aden Author
 Twitter: @eliz_reed_aden
 Instagram: elizabeth_r_aden

AUTHOR WEBSITE:
 www.elizabethreedaden.com
 www.eunicemaysboyd.com

Also by the Authors

Other books by Eunice Mays Boyd
Murder Breaks Trail (1943)
Honorable Mention, 3rd Mary Roberts Rinehart Mystery
Contest
Doom in the Midnight Sun (1944)
Murder Wears Mukluks (1950)

Co-author of:
The Marble Forest by Theo Durant (1950)

Other books by Eunice Mays Boyd and Elizabeth Reed Aden
One Paw Was Red
A Vacation to Die For
Dune House (2021)

Other books by Elizabeth Reed Aden
The Goldilocks Genome
HEPATITIS Beach

Also by EUNICE MAYS BOYD with ELIZABETH REED ADEN

Murder Breaks Trail (1943)

Doom in the Midnight Sun (1944)

Murder Wears Mukluks (1945)

The Marble Forest (1950)

Dune House (2021)

CPSIA information can be obtained
at www.ICGtesting.com
Printed in the USA
BVHW031105200222
629589BV00006B/331